"No one has seen my brother Fallon, Fallon Dean, since the beginning of December last year," she said, diving in. **"Yesterday was the six-month anniversary of his disappearance."**

Detective Lovett put his coffee down and grabbed a pen.

"How old is he?"

"Twenty-three. Twenty-four in September."

"And why are you just coming to us now about this after six months?"

His expression hadn't changed since he'd come into the office. Millie wished she could read what he was feeling. Just like she wished the part of her that wanted to know didn't also find him extremely attractive. That part of her was intrigued by him, despite the situation.

"This isn't the first time I've been here." She hesitated, hoping to find the magic words to keep him from dismissing her. "I reported it the day after he went missing."

"So it's an ongoing investigation?"

Millie shook her head.

"He hasn't been found but the case was technically closed four months ago."

That earned an eyebrow raise. His gaze flitted down to the folders on his desk before he responded.

"A closed case means a concluded case," he stated.

UNCOVERING SMALL TOWN SECRETS

TYLER ANNE SNELL

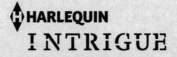

This book is for the readers who have followed my characters
and stories throughout the years. We've just left the Nash family
in Tennessee and now we're meeting a ragtag group of misfits in
small-town Alabama trying their best to make a difference.
I hope you enjoy them all.

HARLEQUIN®
INTRIGUE®

Recycling programs
for this product may
not exist in your area.

ISBN-13: 978-1-335-55518-2

Uncovering Small Town Secrets

Copyright © 2021 by Tyler Anne Snell

This edition published by arrangement with Harlequin Books S.A.

For questions and comments about the quality of this book,
please contact us at CustomerService@Harlequin.com.

Harlequin Enterprises ULC
22 Adelaide St. West, 40th Floor
Toronto, Ontario M5H 4E3, Canada
www.Harlequin.com

Printed in U.S.A.

Tyler Anne Snell genuinely loves all genres of the written word. However, she's realized that she loves books filled with sexual tension and mysteries a little more than the rest. Her stories have a good dose of both. Tyler lives in Alabama with her same-named husband and their mini "lions." When she isn't reading or writing, she's playing video games and working on her blog, *Almost There*. To follow her shenanigans, visit tylerannesnell.com.

Books by Tyler Anne Snell

Harlequin Intrigue

The Saving Kelby Creek Series

Uncovering Small Town Secrets

Winding Road Redemption

Reining in Trouble
Credible Alibi
Identical Threat
Last Stand Sheriff

The Protectors of Riker County

Small-Town Face-Off
The Deputy's Witness
Forgotten Pieces
Loving Baby
The Deputy's Baby
The Negotiation

Orion Security

Private Bodyguard
Full Force Fatherhood
Be on the Lookout: Bodyguard
Suspicious Activities

Manhunt

Visit the Author Profile page at Harlequin.com.

CAST OF CHARACTERS

Foster Lovett—Once a hotshot detective in Seattle, this newest hire has moved back to his hometown to help redeem the sheriff's department from its corrupt past. But it's not until his beautiful new neighbor tries to convince him that her younger brother is in trouble that danger swiftly follows and he realizes the town he left behind has changed in a lot more ways than he ever imagined.

Millie Dean—Everyone thinks her brother ran away but his older sister knows something else is going on. After six months of searching for answers, she hopes the new lead detective at the sheriff's department will listen, but things get complicated fast when she finds herself a target and the attraction between her and Foster becomes undeniable.

Fallon Dean—Younger brother to Millie, this twenty-three-year-old just disappeared one day without any explanation.

Brutus Chamblin—Interim sheriff and family friend to Foster, he's not about to make the same mistakes as his predecessors.

Carlos Park—This deputy is one of the many locals who believe that the Dean family is nothing but trouble.

Lee Gordon—Forced to retire because of an injury inadvertently caused by Fallon, this former detective has the motive to make trouble for the Deans.

Chapter One

Everyone in town went looking for Annie McHale when she first went missing. A year later and only three people went looking for Fallon Dean.

Detective Gordon was the third person to join the search. In his late fifties, he had been a week away from retiring and thought that Fallon had simply run away. But nothing had been that simple in Kelby Creek, Alabama. Not since the scandal known as The Flood had rocked Dawn County and nearly destroyed the small town. So, after conferring with the interim sheriff, he'd been encouraged to extend his stay to make sure nothing bad had happened to the twenty-three-year-old.

It had made the tired, grouchy man even more tired and even more grouchy. He'd done his investigation wearing an expression that looked like he always had a glass of spoiled milk stuck beneath his nose. However, worse than how he asked his questions during the investigation was the less-than-enthused answers he received.

The town had a lot of history it was trying to forget, but Fallon? He'd caused an accident that some weren't ready to let go.

Then there was Larissa Cole.

Before Detective Gordon had been assigned the case, Larissa had been first in line to help. The moment the Dean family had come to Kelby Creek five years prior, she'd taken to them with an open heart and a maternal air that neither Dean sibling had felt in a long while. If she believed Fallon had left town of his own free will, it didn't matter because she was worried, regardless. She had become Millie's best friend and, while she loved Fallon like a brother, it was Millie who was hurting.

And hunting.

It had been six months to the day since Millie Dean had seen her little brother. In the time between first meeting with Detective Gordon to plead the case that something was wrong to now standing in her kitchen, looking out the window into the hot June daylight, only the smaller details had changed.

Fallon's lease on his apartment had expired, and all of his belongings were in Millie's guest bedroom. His cell phone was still paid for but had long since been off, just as his job at the newspaper had been filled. Even the rumor mill had gone on hiatus when it came to the Dean family.

They smiled and waved and had pleasant small

talk with Millie at the grocery store or walking along the sidewalk of the neighborhood. They gave her the traditional Southern nod or half-wave when catching her eye while driving. They said it was about time Detective Gordon retired after only two months of searching, and they sure as the day was humid didn't offer to help look for him, not even on the six-month anniversary of his disappearance.

As far as Kelby Creek was convinced, although he was a grown man, Fallon Dean was a runaway. The name had stuck ever since he ran away as a teenager. And now everyone was convinced he wasn't missing.

Millie fisted her hand against the lemon-printed towel draped over the lip of the sink. Six months and one day ago she would have fretted at wrinkling the fabric. It was for light hand dabbing and decoration. Something she'd bought in the city on impulse because it had matched a sundress she'd once gotten a lot of compliments on at the grocery store.

But now?

Now she crumpled it in her hand like a wet paper towel.

Long gone was the woman in the lemon sundress. In her place had moved the sister who would do anything to find her only family.

Even if that meant starting over again.

She dropped the towel on the counter and

turned on her heel. Her home had been built in the seventies but renovated by the owner before her. Nothing felt vintage about the two-bedroom anymore. It was all clean lines, whites, grays and wood, with accent walls of shiplap here and there.

One of those accent walls stood behind the eat-in table. On that wall was mounted a white board much too large for the space.

Millie traced her own handwriting across its surface.

Then she went to the coffee maker and started a new cup.

It wasn't until her phone rang hours later that she realized it had gone dark outside.

"Hello?"

Millie's stomach growled in tandem with her answering the call. Larissa's voice came through in a rush.

"Zach just called and asked who the man was moving into the rental next to your house. He said there was a moving truck out in front of it at the curb when he drove past to go to church and was still there when he came back."

Millie pushed out of the dining chair she'd nearly grown roots on as she'd gone over every detail of her own investigation into Fallon and made a path back to the kitchen window. A streetlamp stood sentry between her mailbox and the rental house in question, but its light showed an empty road.

"I didn't see a moving truck earlier and I don't see one now. Are you sure Zach saw right?"

There was motion on Larissa's side of the phone. She repeated the question to their co-worker Zach, who must have been in the background. He responded but Millie couldn't hear him.

"He's sure. He said your car was in the driveway both times too so you must have seen him." Larissa paused. Millie could picture the forty-two-year-old perfectly despite the distance between them. Her round face arranging into a harmless, comfort-filled expression, glasses in need of being pushed back up the bridge of her nose and brown eyes that held more maternal concern than Millie or Fallon had ever gotten from their own mother. "What *have* you been up to today?"

Millie only ever felt guilt about her determination to find her brother when she decided to lie to her best friend about how determined she still was. Larissa had tried to take off work to spend the day with Millie, knowing it was the anniversary, but the truth was that Millie had woken up that morning with one goal.

To finally get answers.

No matter what.

Telling that to the levelheaded, good-intentioned mother hen who had seen firsthand how Millie had changed in the last six months?

It only made the worry in Larissa grow from her heart and fan out into her own life.

And Millie didn't want that.

So she lied and said she wanted to spend the day alone, lounging and catching up on her TV shows.

"I've been stuck in TV land all day," she said now. "*Community* has six seasons and I was only on season two. You know I'm a completist when it comes to shows."

There was a hesitation again but then Larissa seemed to accept the fib.

"Well, make sure you get some food in you since I know how you can forget to eat sometimes when you're focused," she said. "I'm still coming over to drop off some cookies after my shift around ten. You better show me some dirty dishes to prove you ate." Larissa's soothing tone switched as quickly as the topic. "Now, go next door and find out who your new neighbor is. It's not every day someone moves *to* Kelby Creek."

They ended the call and Millie looked at the clock. She had a few hours before Larissa's well-meaning check-in.

That was plenty of time to retrace Fallon's last known stops around town before he disappeared.

Millie grabbed her purse and hurried out to the driveway. Just like the moving truck, she barely noticed the man walking parallel to her along the driveway next door, a box in his arms. On reflex she nodded a hello when their eyes met.

The light from his front porch showed him returning the gesture. Millie noted, the way one notes something when your mind was already filled with other pressing matters, the easy facts.

The man was young, at least younger than Mr. Tomlin, the tenant before him, had been. She guessed he was closer to her twenty-eight than Mr. Tomlin's sixty-two. Taller too. Built wider and sturdier if the large box he carried with ease was any indication. Millie couldn't get a good grasp of the color of his hair other than it was lighter than her black, and he had a lot of it. Shoulder length and with a matching beard. It felt hot just looking at it. Then again, it was summer in Kelby Creek. That meant even the night gave little respite from the heat and humidity that plagued South Alabama. Past those quick flashes of detail, Millie didn't stick around to register any more.

She had a brother to find, Southern hospitality be damned.

FOSTER LOVETT HADN'T been back in Kelby Creek since he'd run off and married Regina Becker straight out of high school. Not the smartest thing he'd done in his thirty-two years of life but not the dumbest either. He and Regina had a good five years of married bliss before the dam of young insecurities, naive hopes and work had started to crack between them.

When that thing blew, the next five years of marriage had been all about surviving the flood.

They hadn't.

Now Foster was back in his hometown sweating through his jeans, cursing the mosquitoes and wondering who the woman next door was even though he'd sworn off the opposite sex the moment he'd signed the divorce papers and lost his house, his car and the dog two years ago. Sure, he'd gone on a few dates since that fateful day, but the lesson he'd learned from Regina was still seared into his brain.

Women were trouble.

And the woman who'd all but run and jumped into her car before speeding off? Well, he guessed she might be that with a capital *T*.

Foster was done with trouble. Or at least the woman kind. Professionally he had run back to Kelby Creek and jumped right into the sack with a damned mess. One he hoped he could help clean up.

He hefted the box of dishes high as he opened the front door to his rental home and jostled inside. The AC had been running since that morning, but the air was still on the stale side. He scrunched up his nose at it and slid the box onto the kitchen counter just as his phone started blaring. He eyed the oven's clock. It was almost seven at night.

The caller ID of a man whose first name was honest-to-God Brutus popped up on the touch screen.

Foster straightened and answered.

"Yello."

"Hey there, Love, sorry for calling when you requested some quiet while getting settled," the weathered and deep voice of interim sheriff Brutus Chamblin answered. "But I heard through the grapevine that you were being a grump at Crisp's Kitchen no more than half an hour ago, so I figured you were probably still up to no good."

Foster rolled his eyes and started to open the box he'd just put down.

"I wasn't grumpy, I just wasn't chatty. That's all."

"That's the same thing when you live in a town with only eighteen hundred or so people. You should know that already, or has living big in Seattle made you forget the niceties of being Southern?"

The sigh escaped him faster than the packing tape split on top of the box.

"I moved back to help redeem the image of this town and the sheriff's department. You'd think that would earn me a little leeway when I don't spend a half hour talking to Quinn Cooper about the fish he caught at the creek two months ago while trying to finish my dinner."

Brutus laughed.

Sheriff Chamblin laughed.

Foster was going to have to get used to the idea that his father's old friend was now acting interim sheriff until someone else was elected. That meant giving the man a little more formality than came naturally to him. Especially since Foster was now the lead detective in his department.

"Well, it might not kill you to fake the smiles and interest for a while. At least until things get a little more normal around here."

Foster started to pull out the plates while making a mental note to go out and buy new silverware. After the divorce he'd moved in with a buddy from the Seattle Police Department before segueing into a studio apartment. Somewhere during the different moves he'd lost more and more furniture, odds and ends, and, weirdly enough, forks. For the life of him he had no idea where they'd all gone to.

"I'll see what I can do," he finally said. "Just as long as you remember I'm not here to fake nice. I'm here to solve cases."

"Speaking of which…" Foster paused, plate in midair. He hadn't had an active case in almost two months. Just the thought of one got his blood pumping. There was a rustling on the other side of the phone. "I still don't have anything other than cold cases sitting on your desk. Maybe you can help make sense of at least one of them. Lord knows the people of Kelby Creek could use a win, and with a rock-star detective like you joining our ranks, maybe we can finally get them one."

Foster resumed his unpacking and nodded to himself. He never liked being called a rock star, but he was proud of his above-average closing rate that had made him somewhat famous within his career in law enforcement.

"I'll take a look at them first thing in the morning," he said.

"Good. I'll stop in to check up on you after my meeting with the interim mayor. He thinks since we're both temporary that we should be in constant talks about the town." Brutus sighed this time. "The man could drive a nun to drink, I tell you what."

Foster laughed and adopted the older man's earlier tone.

"Now, now, Sheriff. Don't you go forgetting your Southern niceties."

Brutus grumbled.

"Yeah, yeah. See you in the morning, Love."

The call ended, and Foster spent the rest of the night unpacking. The rental house was a two-bedroom but on the smaller side. At least for the town; for his studio in Seattle? Not so much. It wasn't until he was done that Foster realized the house still looked mostly empty.

It should have bothered him, he thought, but then again, when had he ever been a homebody?

Foster showered and then jumped into bed, mind already on the files that would be sitting on his desk in the morning. It wasn't until a few hours had passed and he got up for a glass of water that he noticed the woman from next door hadn't come home yet.

He wondered who she was again.

"You're wasting your time," he told himself out loud, empty glass in his hand. "You're here to work. Not make nice with the neighbors."

The small reminder was enough. Foster went back to bed. His routine kicked in after that.

He slept. His alarm went off and woke him. He ate. He dressed. He hopped into the used red Tacoma he'd bought a few weeks before and drove to work. His mind took in details around him in quick succession even though his focus was on something he hadn't even read yet.

He nodded to Libby at the front desk, said a few words to a deputy he hadn't formally met yet and passed by Brutus's closed office door before going to the end of the hall and hanging a left.

Detective Lovett was etched on a new nameplate next to one of two doors down the small hallway.

But his door wasn't closed.

In fact, not only was it open, there was someone sitting just inside it across from his desk.

Foster didn't recognize the dark curls, but he did recognize the concerned face as he walked around the stranger to his chair.

It was the woman from the night before. The woman in a hurry.

His neighbor.

"Good morning," he said, adding a question to his greeting. "May I ask who you are and why you're in here?"

With better lighting Foster was able to see just how beautiful the stranger was. Hair as dark as night, a mixed complexion that made her amber eyes even more bright as they took him in, and long angles that made him think of the description of royalty before he could stop it from popping into his head. Her long eyelashes brushed against her brown cheeks as she followed him with her eyes.

The woman gave what, he imagined, was a standard polite smile. But then it wiped clear from her lips. In its place worry so acute it made Foster's spine zip up to attention.

"My name is Millie Dean and I need your help."

Chapter Two

Millie had bribed Libby and Deputy Park with chocolate chip cookies to get back to the detective's office and wait until he arrived. Libby was more than willing to let her back, but Deputy Carlos Park was huffier. He gave her a look she was all too familiar with but eventually took a few cookies back to the bullpen. Whipping up the yummy confections had been an easy price to pay for early access to the back hallway.

After a long night of trying to find the truth in the dark, she'd wound up home, defeated. Larissa had shown up soon after and given her an ounce of hope she hadn't expected to get.

A lead detective had finally been hired to take Detective Gordon's former position.

Which meant Millie had a chance.

And meant she had needed to talk to the new hire as soon as possible.

Yet, after introducing herself, Millie's nerves doubled.

For many different reasons.

First of all, the Dawn County Sheriff's Department wasn't exactly beloved anymore. Not after a thunderstorm and a subsequent flash flood had caused the former mayor to wreck into a ditch. Not after the FBI agent responding to the crash found something that led to uncovering a town-wide conspiracy. Not after the corruption that had hollowed out the town and forced most of the Kelby Creek's high-ranking officials and employees, former sheriff and mayor included, into jail. Or sent some on the run.

The event itself was so widespread and complicated that the entire town nicknamed it The Flood. A name still said with as much anger and deep feelings of betrayal and distrust as it had been the day the news broke of the corruption.

Those who had been involved within the sheriff's department hadn't just broken the law, they'd shattered it. Their actions had given Kelby Creek a bad reputation that stretched countrywide and left the residents with a serious case of trust issues. Even with the new hires and transfers who had slowly been trickling in to restock the department and change its image for the better.

Millie didn't know if that was possible, but it was the reason why she was hopeful. Still, she didn't know the detective and that made her uneasy of itself.

Second, as Millie sat in the department, Fallon's MIA six-month anniversary felt painfully more apparent. Unable to be ignored. All the days between when she'd seen him leaving her house to now had collected together and they hurt. She hadn't gotten good news once, and now she was trying again to have a full-fledged conversation with a man with a badge. Trust or not, that made the vise around her heart squeeze tighter.

Third, and nowhere near the severity level of the other two points, was the realization that the new detective was the same man she'd seen carrying a box into the house next to hers the night before. Which had to mean he was the man who had rented it. Her new neighbor. One with groomed, dark blond hair, forest green eyes, and a jaw that set hard in intensity as she began to explain why she was waiting in his office.

"No one has seen my brother, Fallon Dean, since the beginning of December last year," she stated. "Yesterday was the six-month anniversary of his disappearance."

Detective Lovett put his coffee down and grabbed a pen.

"How old is he?"

"Twenty-three. Twenty-four in September."

"And why are you just coming to us now about this after six months?"

His expression hadn't changed since he'd come into the office. Millie wished she could read what he was feeling and she wished the part of her that wanted to know didn't also find him extremely attractive. That part of her was intrigued by him, despite the situation.

"This isn't the first time I've been here." She hesitated, hoping to find the magic words to keep him from dismissing her. "I reported it the day after he went missing."

"So it's an ongoing investigation?"

Millie shook her head. "He hasn't been found, but the case was technically closed four months ago."

That earned an eyebrow raise. His gaze flitted to the folders on his desk before responding.

"A closed case means a concluded case," he stated.

Millie mentally bit her tongue, stopping herself from going on the offense.

"The detective in charge of the case hit a dead end and gave up," she said carefully. "Fallon is still out there and—"

A knock on the side of the doorframe behind her broke Detective Lovett's attention.

Millie turned to the new face and felt her frown deepen.

Deputy Carlos Park, his dark buzz cut, and muscles sculpted from an obsession with the gym, had eyes only for the detective.

"Hey, Lovett, could I talk to you for a second?"

"I'm in the middle of something," came the smooth baritone. "Can it wait?"

Deputy Park dropped his gaze to Millie's. She

instantly regretted bringing him cookies. He'd helped himself to them and taken several.

"No," he said. "I don't think it can."

The detective's chair rolled backward as he stood. Millie turned in her chair, away from the deputy, fresh anger coursing through her. Lovett's eyebrow rose again in question, but he didn't ask anything of her.

Which was good because she was already spinning a defense to give him when he came back. After Deputy Park tainted the image of her brother. Just like all the rest of the town would, given the chance. That was half of the reason she'd come in so early, hoping to catch the detective first.

A lot of good that had done.

"Be right back."

Millie nodded, tight and quick. It was only after he was out of the room that she realized she'd fisted her hands on her lap. Attractive or not, intriguing or not, new neighbor or not, Millie knew what was most likely going to happen next.

Still, she had hope that Detective Lovett would be different.

That he wouldn't listen to those who had been at the department five years ago. That he would give her, and Fallon, the benefit of the doubt.

People changed all the time. Fallon more than most.

Did some of the town refuse to believe that?

Specifically, those in the department who were still around?

They sure did.

After The Flood, it was like the pot calling the kettle black.

"Sorry for the wait."

Detective Lovett appeared at her shoulder as fast as Millie noted the change in his tone. He apparently was, in fact, no different from the colleagues he'd most likely just spoken to about Fallon.

Millie decided to cut the polite nonsense.

She didn't have time to dance around their past in the hope of being given a clean slate with the new hire.

"You're going to tell me that my brother ran away. That he's been labeled a flight risk. That he's an adult and that he didn't go missing, he just left." The detective kept his face impassive so Millie prodded him. "Am I wrong?"

Lovett threaded his fingers together into a steeple over his desk.

"I'm going off the facts, Miss Dean," he said, voice even. "Fallon has a history of running away, one that started before what happened once y'all moved to Kelby Creek." He looked down at the notepad he'd taken with him when he stepped into the hallway. There were several notes in tight, neat handwriting across the paper. "Four times between the ages of sixteen and eighteen. Then one time here where, in the process of looking for him, a deputy was struck by a car and forced to retire because of the injury." He looked up at her, his eyes a cool mint. "The former detective on the case found no hint of foul play, not to mention you buried the important detail that Fallon left you a note. One that said he was leaving and that he was okay."

The note.

The damned note.

It was the biggest reason no one took her seriously.

That no one listened to her reasoning behind not trusting it.

Now Millie was trying not to yell. Not to raise her voice in the hope that being loud would make him understand.

That it would make him see what she did.

Yet she wasn't fast enough to find the right words before he spoke again.

"You have to understand my reluctance here. Leaving isn't the same as missing."

Millie stood, Detective Lovett did the same. Now she could read him perfectly. He opened his mouth to continue, but Millie held up her hand to stop whatever it was he was about to say.

"You know what? I was an idiot to come here of all places looking for help. After what this department did? I don't know why anyone would ever come here looking for answers."

The detective's jaw hardened. His nostrils flared just enough to show her that she'd hit a nerve.

"What happened to the department, happened," he rebutted. "But that's not who we are now, and we're working very hard to prove that to the community."

"Just like Fallon has worked very hard the last four years to prove he isn't that kid anymore. He's not a thoughtless runaway. That what happened, happened, but that's not who he is now." Millie grabbed her purse and angled her body to the door. She was mad, sure, but she was also hurt.

She was also more than done with the conversation.

She was going to find Fallon.

She was going to save him from whatever bad had happened.

She didn't need the department, certainly not the detective who had judged her and her family without a second thought.

Millie paused in the doorway and cut the man off with a parting shot.

"You've known about Fallon for less than an hour. I've known him for twenty-three years. That note wasn't written by him, and he didn't leave because he wanted to." She almost left then, but six months of not knowing propelled the words out before she could decide against them.

"And not that anyone ever seems to care about

this part but when Fallon ran away when he was younger, it was always because he was running from our stepfather. But our dad is gone and has been for years. That's what scares me now. That's why I came here hoping to get the help of someone without any biases, knowing I'd probably still get turned away. If Fallon ran away of his own accord, then what was he running from this time?"

Detective Lovett didn't answer. He couldn't have even if Millie had given him time to respond.

He didn't know Fallon.

He didn't know her.

And now he never would.

THE COLD CASES on Foster's desk were still just as cold when he left for the day as they had been that morning. Some were from six years ago, others dated back to the late nineties. They were challenging, and he was more than up for each of those challenges.

But he'd be lying to himself if he didn't admit his focus hadn't been 100 percent since Millie Dean had stormed out of his office.

"Check into it if you need to," Deputy Park had said earlier. "But the last time the department went looking for Fallon he was out in the woods smoking pot and eating gummy worms. Because of him Deputy William Reiner was hit by a damn car while searching the county road.

Hear you me, wherever Fallon is, he probably doesn't give a rat's backside that anyone is wasting their time looking for him."

Foster waited a few minutes after Park left before deciding to pull Fallon's file. He placed it on top of the cold cases he was *supposed* to be looking into and read the contents from first page to last during his lunch break.

What Park had summarized in the hallway was most of what was in the files.

Millie Dean had come to the department when she couldn't find her brother over a weekend. All she knew was that his car was gone too and that the note she'd found on her front porch wasn't from him. Detective Lee Gordon had been assigned to the case and, as far as Foster could tell by his language used in writing the report, he had mostly focused on finding the car.

He hadn't found it or Fallon. Not even a trace.

Foster moved the folder off to the side for the remainder of the day but, like the thought of his sister, Foster would catch himself glancing at Fallon Dean's life boiled down into three sheets of a paper and a picture that that same sister had most likely provided.

Foster was an only child, but that didn't mean he was apathetic to Millie's worry. Her pain. His career so far had shown him monsters, victims and survivors. He'd had to deliver devastating news to families just as he'd been able to deliver justice for what happened to them.

He'd also never gotten a case he hadn't closed, even if he didn't like the outcome.

It was the argument his captain in Seattle had used to try to keep him in the zip code.

Every day you're doing real work here. That town? Everyone is already against you before you even put on the badge. It's like quicksand. Wouldn't you rather stay here where you know you can make a difference instead of rolling the dice and hoping for the best?

Foster had answered with what he still believed to be true.

He needed a change of scenery, and what better way than to do that while also trying to help an entire town?

A town that included Millie Dean.

Eyes the color of sunlight shining on syrup.

The same eyes that had pleaded with him before narrowing in anger.

Now, hours later and sitting in his driveway, there Foster was thinking about those eyes again.

It didn't help that the woman herself could be seen through the front window, bustling around inside her house.

Foster didn't mean to, but he stared for a moment and replayed their conversation in his head. Then he did something he'd always done in his career. He put the memory of her from his office on mute and read her body language instead.

Anxious. Worried. Genuine.

She truly believed something was wrong. So much so she'd chanced going to a place she clearly didn't like, knowing there was a good chance she'd be turned away. Regret at that choice had tensed her body right before anger at being dismissed had. Then, before she'd even stood, Foster had realized it was him who had been dismissed.

And he hadn't liked it.

Not one bit.

Foster sighed, locked his truck and went inside his house. Belatedly he realized he could see into one of the woman's rooms from his small kitchen. He decided to avoid that window as he changed out of his dress shirt and slacks and into more comfortable clothes. He checked his email, thought about a few of the cold cases he'd looked into earlier, and finally gave himself permission to put all work matters away long enough to eat.

Corruption and conspiracy aside, it wasn't as though a small town like Kelby Creek was all that exciting. Not like Seattle had been.

So, Foster grabbed a beer, heated up a frozen meal and plopped down on the one chair he had in the dining room with every intention of forgetting about the outside world for a while.

But then he heard his neighbor's front door shut and curiosity made him go to his kitchen window, beer in tow. Millie Dean herself was hurrying out into the darkness to her car.

The motion sensor camera at the corner of her driveway came on.

"Oh hell," Foster breathed out.

Millie had a flashlight in one hand and a baseball bat in the other. She took both into the car with her. Foster put his beer down.

"Well, that can't be good."

Chapter Three

The town of Kelby Creek was a warm place.

From spring to summer to Christmas Eve, there was a good chance its humidity was fogging up your glasses and making you sweat. It was at most times unforgiving.

The night was no different.

Millie's shirt stuck to her skin, her jeans wrapping her thighs with a cling that was wholly uncomfortable. Her curls were a ball of chaos atop her head in a bun, giving her neck the space to sweat openly instead of beneath the weight of her hair. Even the bat in her hand was starting to slide in her grip.

It wasn't pleasant.

Neither was the darkness around her.

The Kintucket Woods acted like a barrier between Kelby Creek and the outside world. Pine trees, oaks and wild underbrush had taken over most of the expansive boundary, but there was one section that Millie knew of that had a clearing.

One wide enough for a tent, a small campfire and a young boy in need of an escape.

Millie had long since left the beams from her headlights behind at the road. Now the flashlight in her other hand showed a path of dirt and roots and nothing else. No footsteps that she could see, no signs of someone else walking the same way.

Not that there was any other sign of life around her either.

The branches and leaves overlapping above hid the moonlight almost completely. Like the light switch had been flipped off on the world around her. It made the usually comforting sound of cicadas and frogs chirping an eerie one.

Millie held down a shiver of anticipation and fear as she marched on, hoping that the second she was at her destination, every worry about Fallon would disappear with his smiling face.

Though she knew it was an impossibly long shot.

You're here because you don't know what to do next, she told herself. Again. *And because this was his safe place.*

Millie took one step into the clearing and felt her hopes crash into the underbrush, despite readying herself for it to be empty.

She still tried. "Fallon?"

Her call fell flat.

There was no Fallon, there was no tent, there

weren't even signs that a fire had once been used for warmth, light and a few s'mores.

She had hoped it would be that simple.

That Fallon had gone off on his own and now realized it was time to come home.

But it wasn't that simple.

Just like asking for help at the sheriff's department hadn't been simple either.

Detective Lovett had done exactly what Millie had been afraid he'd do. He hadn't listened.

Millie let out a defeated breath and moved closer to the center of the clearing.

If Fallon wasn't here, then where was he?

She let her gaze unfocus and let her mind wander. She propped the bat against her leg. The weight of mental exhaustion weighed her down.

But not so much as to keep her from jumping when a rustling sounded behind her.

Millie spun, taking her bat up again, and let the flashlight's beam scatter among the trees to her right. For a moment she expected to see her tall, dark and smiling pain-in-the-butt brother but, for a second time that night, her hopes were dashed.

Then fear took their place.

The man was tall and wispy. Like the wind could take him if it blew hard enough. He had on a pair of dark green coveralls and orange work boots. His dark hair was shaved close to his head. Millie guessed he might have been in his midthirties. What she couldn't guess was why he was out here, of all places, and at night.

Staring at her like he wasn't surprised that she was there.

Millie took a step back but kept the flashlight beam on his body.

He smiled. "Don't worry. I'm not going to hurt you," he greeted. His voice was stronger than he looked. "You work at Dobb's, right?"

Millie nodded on reflex.

She didn't recognize him from the grocery at all.

"I saw you there last week," he continued. "You had one of those big orange clips in your hair. Reminded me of my mom."

He took another step forward then stopped. A smile pulled up a corner of his mouth. Millie gripped the bat tighter. There was enough light in the clearing to lose the flashlight if she had to, but if she ran into the woods without it, she'd be in trouble.

Still, she readied to do it all the same.

Drop the flashlight.

Put both hands into swinging the bat with all the power that she had.

Run only after he was down and out for the count.

"Who are you?" she asked. There was no tremble in her voice, but there was also no emotion in it. The man's eyebrow rose.

"I'm just trying to be a friend is all." His smile vanished. "I'm looking for Fallon. But it doesn't look like he's here. Just you."

That put a temporary hold on her fear.

"You know Fallon?"

The man nodded slowly. "We go way back. I thought it was high time I do my part and help look for him. Because I don't know where he is." The man started to walk forward. "And I'd really like to."

The fear came back.

Millie felt like she'd been zapped by lightning. Every nerve in her came to life with a pulse of energy and one thunderous boom of thought.

No one knew she was out in the woods.

Not Larissa. Not Fallon.

No one.

Suddenly she saw what her trek into the woods alone was. Desperation of a terrified heart. Desperation that had led her into the darkness without a soul in the world knowing where she was.

Annie McHale's smiling face popped up into Millie's head, followed by Fallon.

Just another disappearance in the town of Kelby Creek.

So, Millie did the only rational thing left to do in the irrational situation she'd already gotten herself into.

She swung the bat with all she had.

Then she ran.

FOSTER LOST MILLIE right outside the neighborhood. One second he was watching her book it out to the main road and the next he was following her in his truck.

But she was fast and had a lead on him.

Once she was out of the neighborhood, it was like the world had gone to sleep.

He sat idling at the corner of Melrose Street and Lively Drive, trying to figure out which way the woman had gone. There was no car, no headlights and no Millie Dean behind the wheel, damn determined to do *something*.

Something with a bat.

Which was not good.

Foster looked off to his right. He mentally traced the road to the heart of town. He turned to his left and looked out at the street as it slipped off into darkness.

Not only did Millie have a bat, but she also had a flashlight.

She was going somewhere she didn't feel safe and somewhere she needed light.

The woods.

Nothing good ever happened at night in the woods.

What Kelby Creek lacked in big-city amenities and attractions, it more than made up for in back roads that looked straight out of a horror movie. Networks like reaching fingers branched off from the street Foster was on and led to the woods and the town limits. Some had older streetlamps, marking roads of gravel and dirt. Most had nothing but the moonlight to show their paths.

When Foster and his friends had been teenagers, they'd been fans of the twisting darkness with its almost-secret roads. It made their field and creek parties and hangouts private and easier to get away with when the law inevitably came to break them up. Or someone's parents. It was almost comical watching cars filled with teens scattering down different roads while the adults tried to remember from their own youth which roads led to where. Yet, as one of those adults now—and law enforcement too—Foster saw what a pain in the backside the most rural part of Kelby Creek really was.

It took him almost fifteen minutes to find the road that Deputy Park had said led to the clearing Fallon had been found in years ago. The same road that led to the spot where William Reiner had been struck by a car, effectively ending his career.

Foster should have found the road much sooner but he didn't.

And, when he saw Millie's car parked on a patch of grass along the shoulder, he hoped the delay wouldn't cost him. Foster didn't think Fallon was in trouble, but he couldn't deny his curiosity and concern had slowly turned into a sense of urgency.

One that pulled him out of his truck with his service weapon in his holster, his badge around his neck and his cell phone tucked into the pocket of his jeans. He didn't know what was going on, but he planned to ask Millie when he found her.

When he found her *safe* and sound.

Yet, no sooner had he thought about a potentially angry Millie asking why he was there than something happened that sent his sense of urgency blasting through the roof.

A scream split the night air.

A woman's scream.

It was brief but loud, carrying through the trees and up to Foster like a wave coming to shore.

He was off and into the darkness without a second thought.

Bark bit into his palms as he slapped his hands against the trees he passed, trying to keep from stumbling without losing his momentum. The light from the night sky left him wanting. Just like the flashlight on his truck's floorboard.

The gun in his holster was heavy against his hip.

Pulling it out now would only run the chance of accidentally harming Millie, and he wasn't going to risk that.

Foster kept on his trajectory for a few more seconds before realizing the world had quieted again. He slowed, tilting his head and trying to figure out where Millie was. When he heard nothing new, he called out.

"Millie?"

It didn't take long after that.

Something in the distance started crashing through the underbrush. Foster couldn't tell if it was coming to him or away from him but he strode out, ready to chase if needed.

"It's Detective Lovett," he yelled out. "With the sheriff's department!"

Whoever was making the ruckus ahead of him was keeping a distance between them despite the call. Foster might have grown up in Kelby Creek, but he was in uncharted territory at the moment. He tried to pull up a mental map of the area to figure out where Millie was running to or where the person who made her scream might be headed, but he was coming up short. There were too many variables and he had no idea what was going on even if there hadn't been.

That only became clearer as something barreled between the trees from behind him.

Foster skidded to a stop and pivoted, muscles already in overdrive.

In the dark he could barely make out the dark eyes of Millie Dean, wide and searching. The soft click of a flashlight caused the immediate area to come to life.

Millie had a sheen to her skin and a look that

said she was somewhere in her flight or fight mode. She no longer had her bat.

When she spoke her words were strained and low.

"Wh-why are you out here?" she whispered.

Foster didn't have time to explain. He could still hear someone behind him running away. That had to be the reason Millie screamed. So he pivoted the conversation too.

"Why did you scream?" he asked. "Who attacked you?"

Millie's eyebrows turned into each other. Shadows transformed her look of panic into one of confusion. She titled her head to the side in question.

"I didn't."

Foster matched her confusion.

"You didn't get attacked?" he asked. "Then why did you scream?"

Before Millie could even say another word, Foster knew without a doubt that his first week back in Kelby Creek was about to get more complicated.

Millie shook her head. A bead of sweat slid down her cheek as she answered.

"I didn't scream. Which means there's someone else in danger in these woods."

Chapter Four

"You weren't kidding when you said you were itching to get to work, huh?"

Sheriff Chamblin had his badge pinned to his belt and sleep in his eye. He'd also donned a pair of cowboy boots, something Foster hadn't seen the man do since he was a teen watching Chamblin and his dad heading out to go fishing.

The image was at first a flash of comfort, thinking of his father. Then that badge reminded him that the time between then and now had stretched and twisted. Chamblin was in charge and Foster wasn't some rebellious teen anymore. His expertise was valuable to the sheriff.

Even if that expertise wasn't exactly getting any answers at the moment.

"I told you when I came aboard that I was going to be as transparent as a thin sheet of plastic," Foster answered. "So here I am. Thin sheet of plastic."

Foster swept his arms out wide with the tree line behind him. His truck hadn't moved since he'd parked it two hours ago, and neither had Millie's Nissan. The only change of scenery was the addition of the sheriff and a patrol car with two deputies who didn't look any more enthused than they had when they'd first been called in.

Which was to say not at all.

Apparently Deputy Park wasn't the only deputy with trust issues when it came to the Dean family.

Now the sheriff moved his gaze to the woods right before a deep sigh rumbled out. Whether it was the poor lighting from his headlights or because the man had obviously just been woken up, Chamblin looked much older than he had that morning.

"So no one could find the woman who screamed."

It was a statement and one that Foster didn't like agreeing with.

"I couldn't find the man Millie said she talked to either," Foster added. "But I found a pretty decent footprint in the clearing. I took a few pictures while Deputy Park and Deputy Juliet looked around. But you know as well as I do that the Kintucket Woods are a beast all their own. I need a better search party."

Chamblin shook his head then lowered his voice.

"You think the woman who screamed is still out here somewhere?"

"I wish I knew," Foster said. "But if she isn't

out there, then there's a good chance the man could have taken her. Which is even more reason for us to look for evidence or something that could lead us to one or the other." Foster let his voice drop so low that the sheriff leaned in to hear better when he continued. "As far as the public is concerned, this could be another Annie McHale situation in the making. A woman, now missing, in trouble in the woods? They'll eat this up if we don't handle it with every bit of attention we have."

The sheriff didn't like that.

"This is only an Annie McHale situation if I was the one to kidnap the girl and everyone and their dang mamas helped cover it up. And I sure as hell didn't do that," he said with a shake of his head. Disgust. Written across his expression just as it had been in his voice at the press conference announcing his acceptance of the role of interim sheriff. Anyone who respected the law and the duty to protect their people had deep anger and disbelief at those who had put Kelby Creek on the map for the worst reasons.

It was still a sore subject to the sheriff now.

Movement came from Millie's car. Before the deputies had shown up she'd been at Foster's side, helping him search the immediate area and clearing while recounting her conversation with the man in the coveralls. He'd already sent a description to the department but, like the deputies he spoke with in person, he'd been met with a hesitation once Millie's name came out. Since the deputies had shown up she'd gone to her car. Now she opened the door and stepped out. Yet she kept her distance.

Chamblin smiled her way but stayed in their conversation.

"We have no evidence that a crime was committed and a witness who has been labeled as suspect," he said matter-of-factly. "What if it was Millie Dean who screamed? What if she lied to you, Love?"

Foster had already had the thought. He wouldn't be a good detective if he hadn't.

Had Millie screamed? And if so, why?

To distract him from whoever was running through the trees?

Or had what made her scream been something she wished to keep secret?

It was easy to hope that everyone was good and honest, but the harder pill to swallow was to admit that everyone lied about something.

The question now became: Was Millie Dean lying about this?

Foster could give the answer he hoped was true but decided to play devil's advocate instead.

"And what if she didn't lie?"

Chamblin nodded. "Even if we wanted to, we can't ignore this. Not after Annie McHale." The sheriff pulled his phone back out. "Tell Juliet and

Park to keep searching. I'll call Rudy in since he's pretty familiar with the area to help go over it again. I'd call in our K-9 unit to be fast but, well, there isn't one anymore."

"Another repercussion of Kelby Creek's fall from grace," Foster muttered. Chamblin nodded.

"Send Millie home but tell her to come in tomorrow to make an official statement. No use losing more sleep tonight."

"I can go in with Rudy when he gets here," Foster offered. Rudy Clayborn was the oldest deputy on the Dawn County Sheriff's Department's roster and an expert hunter. He had been longtime friends with Patricia Stillwater, the reigning champion of all things nature in Kelby Creek before him.

Before The Flood.

Now she was buried in the Kelby Creek Memorial Cemetery and Rudy was their go-to man when it came to combing the woods.

"Sounds like a plan," the sheriff responded, eyes trailing to his phone.

Foster felt the excitement of a plan start to unfurl within him. Plans either worked out or didn't. Either way, they got results. Still, Foster paused before enacting the new one.

"By the way, what's your take on her and her brother?" he asked. "Everyone at the department seems to already have an opinion."

It was easy to see what the others thought of

the Dean family, but Chamblin had always been an introspective and politically conscious man. He didn't stir any pots unless he was sure of their ingredients.

The sheriff sighed, chest deflating. A look of sympathy folded into his expression.

"Whatever Fallon Dean did or didn't do, the fact is that there's always been one person who couldn't avoid the fallout." He glanced over to Millie. "And she's still standing. I surely won't be the one who tries to knock her down, so I'm going to keep doing my job. We need to get this all figured out ASAP."

It was a good answer. It was also the end of their conversation.

Foster went to the woman still standing.

Dark eyes watched his every move until he stopped across from her.

"We're going to keep searching this place, but you're free to go home," he told her. "I just need you to come into the department tomorrow to make an official statement. The sooner the better."

"I work at the grocery store tomorrow but not until lunch," she said with a nod. "I can come in in the morning."

"Good. That'll work."

A moment of quiet fell between them. Millie looked unsure of something and Foster could feel his own questions trying to convince him to interview her fully right now on the spot. But *unsure* wasn't the only feeling that came across her expression. Foster could tell she was tired, afraid and worried.

So, he decided to wait until the next day to dig deep.

He might not have known Millie Dean, but something in his gut told him although she was trouble with a capital *T*, she wasn't malicious.

He hoped he could trust her.

"I'll see you in the morning," he added after a stock smile.

Foster started to turn but a hand stayed his elbow. When he looked back at the woman, she dropped her touch and met his gaze.

"I was hoping Fallon would be here, that he had really just gone on his own six months ago and had finally decided to come back on the anniversary. He's an artist, so I thought he might try to be poetic about it. But I knew deep down that he wouldn't be there. Still, it was nice to have hope." Millie's body tensed visibly. She glanced toward the trees, then back. "I don't understand why that man was out there looking for Fallon tonight, but I don't think he was out there looking for hope."

She smiled.

It was flash-in-the-pan quick.

Then she was getting into her car.

"I'll see you tomorrow, Miss Dean," he called after her.

She nodded through the window.

Foster didn't watch her go, but he couldn't deny there was a new weight against his chest as he heard the tires grind against the dirt.

His job wasn't to find Fallon Dean.

It wasn't his job to help Millie either.

He had to focus instead on the newest mystery to find its way to Kelby Creek.

The woman who screamed in the woods and the man who tried to attack a woman in the dark.

Not trying to heal Millie Dean's heart.

THUNDER RUMBLED IN the distance. Not enough to wake her, had she been sleeping, but there was enough power in the rumble that it rattled the old window next to her bed.

Millie rolled onto her side and stared at the glass.

It needed a good cleaning.

Just like the rest of the house.

The closer the anniversary had gotten, the more Millie had focused on everything but what should have been normal.

The window needed a good cleaning, but *she* needed Fallon home and safe.

Millie sighed along her pillowcase. Her alarm clock's digital readout let her know that if she stayed where she was, she'd see light of day splaying across her mint-green walls in less than three hours.

Another rumble and rattle of thunder made her mentally amend that conclusion.

A storm was on the way.

And Millie wasn't going to stay in bed, hoping sleep would take her.

She admitted defeat, sat up and placed her bare feet on the floor. The hardwood was cold. Goose bumps pricked up the sides of her arms.

Her mother used to hate having cold feet. So much so that her mom had a pair of socks in almost every room of their home growing up. It had been a point of teasing from Millie's father. He'd often joked that some people hated getting socks for Christmas but for Maryellen Dean, it was one of the best presents a person could be lucky enough to get.

Millie flexed her feet against the floor.

The only socks in her house were tucked tightly in her dresser.

The cold didn't bother her anymore.

She stood against the weight of being tired and grabbed her robe from the end of the bed. It was soft against her arms. She decided to pair its comfort with a cup of coffee and one of the leftover cookies she'd baked.

What a waste that had been. She wished she'd never offered the cookies to Deputy Park.

Millie had never been particularly afraid of the dark, but she couldn't deny she was clumsier in it. She had night-lights with built-in sensors plugged into a few different sockets throughout the house. The one in the hallway blinked on as she walked past. Normally she would have used the light to guide her into the kitchen, but something pulled her across the hallway instead.

The door to the guest bedroom was always open. Everything Fallon owned was either boxed up or in plastic tubs within the space. Millie could have closed the door, compartmentalized Fallon's disappearance by physically putting something between her and everything that reminded her of him.

But she couldn't.

Millie knew every object in the room by now like the back of her hand. What she wasn't familiar with was the sight out the window.

The window that pointed toward her neighbor's house.

Foster Lovett. Detective.

She walked to the window and looked out into the night. She could just make out the porch light from the front of the house. The garage was built into the opposite side, and she couldn't tell if his truck was in the drive.

Did that mean he was still working?

Was he still out in the woods?

The night-light in the hallway turned off.

Millie pulled her robe closer around her, the prickling sense of something being wrong making her want more comfort.

The sound of the woman screaming had been a vivid, haunting sound. A slap to the face in the quiet. A warning and call for help all at once.

Millie had gone to the woods in frustration, desperation and, like she'd told the detective, wanting nothing more than to feel hope. Even for a short while.

She'd left those same woods with three people caught in her mind.

The man in the coveralls, the woman who screamed and Detective Lovett.

Lightning forked high in the sky. The thunder that came next was louder than before.

Millie hoped they found the woman before the storm arrived.

She took a deep breath, but it caught in her throat.

Adrenaline moved through her faster than the lightning had the sky.

The hallway night-light was back on.

But Millie hadn't moved an inch.

Chapter Five

Throw everything.

It was the second thought that ran through Millie's head the moment he stepped into the doorway.

The man from the woods.

The man in the coveralls.

And he was smiling.

Throw *everything.*

Millie's body went on autopilot.

It wasn't like being in the woods—this was her *home.* It was in the middle of the night. He was inside without an invitation.

Apart from those terrifying facts, the man was *close.*

Millie's home wasn't tiny, but the guest bedroom seeming to have shrunk to the size of the jail cell the second the man had filled the doorframe.

Unlike being in the woods together, this time Millie had only two escape routes. The door he was blocking and the closed—and locked—window behind her that she wouldn't have time to open and exit through.

Their close proximity with no options of an easy plan meant the odds of him hurting Millie faster than she could defend herself were high.

She just hoped the same could be said for him.

Millie pulled the lamp off the nightstand in one quick tug. The force of adrenaline pumping through her veins made the throw that came next count.

The man grunted, seemingly caught off guard, but Millie didn't wait to see what damage she might or might not have done. There wasn't time for that. The second the lamp was airborne she had a thick, hardback book in her hands. She didn't even see the title of it before it too was a weapon soaring through the air toward its target.

The man cussed loudly. He staggered forward but not enough for her to get by him. Millie rolled over the bed to force distance between them, already reaching for something else to throw or brandish like a weapon.

"You little bitch," the man ground out. "I just want to know where he is!"

The closest thing to Millie was a garbage bag of clothes that hadn't fit in the closet. It wasn't ideal, but her motto was anything could turn into a weapon with enough willpower.

Though her practicality paled in comparison

to the physical reality she saw as the man flipped the light switch on.

Millie squinted against the sudden brightness, but it was her stomach that twisted at the change in lighting the most.

The man in the coveralls had a gun in his hand, something she definitely hadn't noticed before.

This time she froze. If she hadn't been so scared, she might have felt silly for realizing she'd fought a gun with a lamp.

"Got your attention now, don't I?" the man growled. There was blood at the corner of his mouth. Maybe she'd counted out how effective the lamp could be too soon.

"I—I don't know where Fallon is," Millie responded, voice breaking from the new, insane rush of adrenaline at seeing his gun. "You can search the house and see he isn't here."

The man snarled. It reminded Millie of an angry cartoon character. He didn't seem real. A stranger standing in her house with a gun pointed at her… It didn't seem real.

As if he heard her thoughts, he shook the weapon. He was *too close* to her. There was no way she could fight or flight without running the risk of being hit by a bullet.

"You know," he started, "I asked around about you, about Fallon, and the town really doesn't seem to like either. Well, mostly him. They just seem to feel sorry for you. But, believe you me, they all agree on one thing and that's that you two were inseparable." He shook his head and winced at the movement. Maybe the book had done some damage too. "He may not be here, but I don't believe for a second that you don't know where Fallon is."

The man took a step forward. Millie clutched the bag of clothes against her chest. It was heavy, but wasn't a match for a bullet.

"I've been looking for him," Millie stated, eyes unable to stay off the gun. "Since the day he left, I've been looking. I have no idea where he is."

The man sighed.

He was frustrated; that much she could tell. Almost annoyed, even.

"You know, at first I believed that you really had no idea where he was." He used the gun to motion to the window. "I kept waiting for you to do something suspicious or out of character to show me you were putting on a show for the town, but you didn't. You just went on your boring way doing meaningless and routine things." His smile came back. There was no mirth, just vindication. A man who had won a bet and was about to collect his prize. "*Then* you went to the sheriff's department. And suddenly there you were rushing off into the woods."

A cold, creeping feeling threaded through Millie's stomach.

He'd been watching her, and not just that night.

"I went out there looking for Fallon," she told him. "I was hoping he was there but he wasn't. You saw that!"

The man shook his head again. That frustration was growing. His finger was so close to the trigger of the gun.

"I think you were meeting up with him and I interrupted too soon. So, now, we're going to try this again because I'd really like to get out of here." He readjusted the aim of the gun. This time it was pointing to her head. "Where is your brother and how do we get ahold of him?"

It shouldn't have happened, of all the times for it to surface, it shouldn't have done it there. Yet, standing with a bag of Fallon's forgotten clothes against her and staring at a stranger who very well could kill her, Millie felt it.

Anger.

Red-hot, unbridled anger.

No one was ever going to believe her, were they?

The town, the sheriff's department, even the newcomer detective couldn't take a beat to listen to her.

To hear her out.

To believe the words that she said.

Was that just her destiny?

To be the woman no one ever trusted?

That anger turned to indignation in one blink.

If no one wanted to believe she was telling the truth, then maybe it was time to start lying.

"Okay. Okay." Millie dropped her voice to an almost-whisper. Defeated. "I'll—I'll tell you what I know but only if you put the gun away. I'll just end up blubbering like a baby soon if you don't."

The man snorted.

"You have me cornered," she pointed out. "And all I have is laundry. *Please*."

To Millie's utter surprise, the man obliged. He dropped the gun into his front coverall pocket.

He must have really wanted to know where Fallon was.

But so did she.

Millie took a slow step to the edge of the bed. It put her right across from him.

"Where is he?" he asked.

Millie's palms started to sweat. Her already-racing heartbeat went into overdrive.

She had a plan.

And it was probably a bad one.

"Not here."

Millie charged the man so fast that he didn't have time to do much other than put up his hands. It was a useless defense as she crashed into them, the bag of clothes acting as a bumper between their bodies. The force and momentum dragged and pushed them backward into the opened door.

Millie heard a *crack* but didn't want to stick around to see if that was from the man or the door.

The second his body was flat against the wood she let go of the bag and darted out to the left and into the hallway.

The night-light flashed on and, five steps later as she turned into the living room, a gunshot screamed behind her.

Millie wasn't sure if she screamed too, but by the time she made it to the front door her legs felt like Jell-O and any plan she had of escape dropped through the floor along with her stomach.

Her phone was in the bedroom.

Her car keys were in the kitchen.

A man ready to shoot her would have a clear shot if she didn't clear the porch in seconds.

She barely had time to register that the front door was already cracked as she grabbed the doorknob and yanked it all the way open.

Time seemed to freeze as two forest green eyes stared back at her, the porch light making his long hair almost shine and the gun in hand glint.

Detective Lovett didn't wait for an explanation or warning, which was good, since Millie didn't have time to give either.

The best they could do boiled down to the detective using his strength to push her to the side like he was the strongest man on Earth while Millie didn't resist.

She fell against wooden porch, pain radiating from her knees.

Then it happened.

An awful explosion of sound pierced her ears, followed immediately by another.

Gunshots.

Two gunshots.

Millie closed her eyes tight, knowing that even though the detective had pushed her out of the way, the bullet had still found her.

Yet no blinding pain came.

No darkness either.

Instead, she heard the sound of a falling body.

Scratch that.

Two bodies falling.

Millie opened her eyes and turned back to Foster. She gasped.

Detective Lovett was on the ground.

And he wasn't moving.

BEFORE HE'D EVEN set foot on Millie Dean's front porch, Foster had blamed his slow gut on sentimentally and nostalgia.

He'd spent the last few hours trying to see the same Kelby Creek he'd known growing up. Not seeing the town for what it had become after what had happened to Annie McHale. After The Flood. Not for what it was now.

He'd waited for Rudy, and then they'd gone over the stretch of woods that made up their surroundings only to find one more set of footprints. It wasn't a lot to go on but he hadn't wanted to stop.

Rudy, however, was tired. And not in the same sense as the sheriff had been.

He was the kind of tired that dragged every part of him down. Even his smile. Foster had seen that before in his career, and he'd seen the same look in the mirror once or twice. A part of Rudy had been hollowed out by the world and, sometimes, that hollow part got filled by the bad stuff that came after.

Rudy had seen bad and he'd also lost someone close to him because of it.

And, in those woods, he'd been tired.

Tired and ready to leave when they hadn't found much at all.

Foster empathized with him, but not the deputies who had been helping.

They weren't interested in finding the woman or the man. They had cleared the woods and announced they were going home the second their boots made it past the tree line and to their cruiser.

"Maybe you should ask Miss Dean tomorrow why she came out here with a bat tonight," Deputy Kathryn Juliet had suggested with a grin that had no right to be pulling up the corners of her mouth.

It had made Foster angry. Not just at another attack on Millie but for the fact that this wasn't the sheriff's department that he'd known growing up. The ones who were left hadn't really stayed.

Their hearts didn't seem in it anymore. To Foster, it seemed like they were one foot out the door already.

If it wasn't a cut-and-dry case, then what was the point?

Annie McHale and The Flood had broken them.

But that's why you're here, he had tried to remind himself. *To help them. To find redemption.*

Foster had hoped that he was just being overdramatic, but he had driven away from those woods tangled up in his own thoughts and memories about what used to be and what was.

About wanting nothing more than to leave the town he'd grown up in and then leaving the good life he'd made as an adult behind so he could come back.

It wasn't until he had been turning into the neighborhood that his gut and his head had finally shaken hands and reintroduced themselves to each other.

The man in the coveralls had gone into the woods to ask Millie where her brother was.

But, if Millie had been telling the truth about not knowing him or even recognizing him, then how had he known she was there?

Foster's grip had tightened around the steering wheel as he'd answered himself out loud.

"He followed her, just like you did, Foster."

Foster had cursed beneath his breath and

turned his headlights off. His gut had sent a shot of urgency through him. He'd pulled to the curb instead of into his driveway.

The neighborhood had been quiet. Thunder rumbled as he reached for his gun.

A part of him might have worried that he was being dramatic, that the red flags that had sprung up was just him looking for a lead because he hadn't found much in the woods, but then lightning had split through the night air and Foster had seen it.

Millie Dean's front door was open.

Not by a whole lot but by too much for a house in the dark.

That had been enough for him.

He had reached into his back seat, grabbed what his former partner in Seattle had dubbed the Just in Case. He'd been haphazardly handling it as he'd hurried out of the truck and down the sidewalk toward the front porch.

Then the gunshot had helped him become something he hadn't in a long while.

He'd become calm.

Absolutely and 100 percent calm.

From drawing his gun, to Millie appearing wide-eyed in front of him, Foster had left his sense of urgency and found the only thing that would help him and Millie.

Focus.

So, as his gut let him know he should have realized Millie had still been in danger sooner, his head had taken over.

He'd moved Millie out of the way and pulled the trigger so the man couldn't.

But he had.

Foster's focus had gone and his gut and his head had quieted as the world went dark.

Chapter Six

The rain finally came.

It hit the tin roof and sounded like hail instead of water droplets. Then he could hear the water spreading over the grass behind him. It was soothing, in a way. White noise attached to the irreplaceable scent of rain.

Then there was something else.

Strawberries?

Foster opened his eyes.

Light poured around dark, wild hair and the body of a woman leaning over him. For a moment, Foster forgot where he was, and it was just him looking into the amber eyes of someone concerned.

But then the pain in his ribs said, "How do you do?" and the memory of the gunman poured in faster than the rain falling around them.

"Is he down?" Foster grunted as he tried to sit up. "Wa-was he alone?"

Millie had a phone to her ear and, despite her

darker complexion, looked pale. She also looked relieved.

"He's dead," she told him. Then into the phone, "No! Detective Foster isn't dead. He's awake now." He could hear someone on the other end of the phone call talking quickly. Millie nodded then handed over the phone. She helped him sit up as he grunted out his name, his position and the bare-bone facts to a dispatcher.

He'd shot and killed a man who had the intent to shoot Millie in her own home. He'd taken a bullet after giving out his own.

Normally Foster would have stayed on the phone, but he wanted answers. And he suspected the second that Sheriff Chamblin found out what happened, he would be shooing Foster to the hospital for a checkup.

Foster wanted to take advantage of his alone time with Millie before that.

He ended the call with an apology and a promise not to leave.

Millie didn't seem to approve. She'd run a gauntlet of expressions while watching him talk. From concerned to lost to an impassiveness that smoothed her face and downturned her lips. She took her phone, the same one she'd run back inside to get once the detective had fallen, back from him but her gaze had fallen to his chest.

"The man. He shot you." Her voice softened tenfold. "I thought you were dead."

She reached out but didn't touch where the bullet had hit.

Which was good because it hurt like hell.

If Foster didn't have a set of bruised ribs, then he certainly had some cracked ones. Not to mention the throbbing pain at the back of his head, letting him know that he definitely had hit the floor after being knocked out by the impact of the shot.

Still, he'd been lucky as hell.

"And that's why I always keep Just in Case in my vehicle." He ran his hand over his bulletproof vest, grateful that he'd thrown it on when he did. Millie didn't look as appreciative. She eyed his side where the straps weren't fastened.

"It's not all the way on. You could have been killed."

Foster put his hands against the wood floor of the porch and pushed himself up. Millie stood with him, helping him to steady.

"There wasn't enough time."

Millie didn't seem to like that answer. He heard his own voice soften this time. "And his bullet hit exactly where it needed to, okay? I'll be all right, just sore."

The woman nodded.

"Now, what about you?" he asked, looking her up and down. As far as he could tell, she wasn't injured but, then again, she also had a robe on that covered most of her body. "Did he hurt you?"

She was quick to shake her head.

"No. But I hurt him."

Millie stepped him through the story of what happened from the time she got out of bed until she made it out onto the front porch. In between her recounting of the events and walk-through of the house, Foster made sure to keep himself between her and the man's body, shielding her from seeing him any more than she already had.

Much like the attacker, Foster's bullet had found the man's chest. However, unlike Foster, he hadn't had a vest to protect him.

Now he was bleeding across Millie Dean's hardwood and pink-and-blue rug, looking as out of place in the otherwise cheery home as the gun he'd discarded.

It was only when they were back on the front porch, the man's gun now in Foster's hand, that Millie underlined her biggest takeaway from what had happened.

"He was looking for Fallon," she said. "That was the only thing he was interested in. Fallon."

Her voice had gone small, nearly getting lost in the rain. Foster didn't like how it made him feel to hear it. Just like he was in no way a fan of the still-there anger for her attacker sitting against his chest.

"Is this the first time anyone has ever come to you looking for him?" he asked. "Any friends, enemies, or family?"

He could tell Millie was trying not to look back into her house. To the body on the floor.

"No. He had a few friends here before Annie McHale went missing. After that, like a lot of people, they ended up moving. I reached out to them when he first disappeared, but none have responded. As for enemies? Well, there's a town full of people who think he's an attention-seeking, self-involved guy with nothing better to do than waste everyone's time." Her words had a sharp edge to them. She caught herself and spoke more evenly when she continued. "And family? That's me. Just me."

For the first time since he'd met Millie Dean, Foster realized he didn't know if she had her own family aside from Fallon. Were there wedding pictures hanging on the walls that he'd missed? An engagement ring in a dish next to her bed? A boyfriend who she was hoping to call the second she could?

Surely a woman as beautiful as Millie had someone who would want to know she was okay.

Foster cleared his throat.

"Do you need to call someone? To let them know you're okay before this hits the news and gossip mill?"

Millie shook her head. The movement was as small as her voice.

"Normally I would have called Fallon."

Foster reached out and gently touched her

shoulder. Pain at the move radiated up his side, but he held his expression firm.

"Well, I'm here," he said. "And we'll get to the bottom of this, okay?"

Dark eyes, searching and hard, traced his face. Whatever Millie Dean was looking for in him, he didn't know but she did nod.

"Okay."

THE SUNRISE CRESTED over Haven Hospital's well-kept but extremely small building hours later. The hospital was nestled between a flat park with a couple of benches and one grill and a town limits sign that had seen better days. However, the private hospital was pristine.

It had been created by the McHale family back in the eighties and had been one of the many gems they were proud to have their wealthy names on. But once their daughter had gone missing and then everything had gone from bad to worse to unfathomable, the McHale family had sold their shares in it.

Foster hadn't been to Haven since he was a teen. If the change in majority ownership had resulted in a remodel, he'd been gone too long to recognize any big changes.

All he knew was that while the sun was rising over the hospital, the morgue in the basement looked almost identical to every morgue he'd seen throughout his career.

Concrete. Cold. Weirdly bright.

Then there was the coroner. She was less standard with her blue-streaked black hair, bejeweled lab coat, and gum that she was smacking on as she introduced herself as Amanda Alvarez.

She pointed to the man on the metal table between them. His clothes were gone, in their place a white sheet that was giving off a powerful disinfectant spray smell. The doctor, who Foster didn't know much about other than she was a new hire after The Flood and that she was in her midthirties, motioned to Coveralls.

"So Sheriff Chamblin said he wanted me to call you if anything weird pops while I'm dealing with this one."

"Yeah, I'm working the case," Foster said. "But I'll admit, I didn't think you'd call me in here this quickly, especially since we know what killed him."

Dr. Alvarez's dark eyebrow rose.

"And I didn't expect for you to get here this quick. What were you doing? Sitting in the parking lot waiting?"

Foster sighed. The pain in his side moved with it.

"The sheriff finally convinced me to get examined. I was upstairs finishing the paperwork when you called." Alvarez still had her eyebrow raised in question. Foster motioned to the man between them. "He shot me."

The doctor looked him up and down.

"I've seen a lot of gunshot victims, and I have to say you should get a gold star for how you've fared."

Foster snorted. "I was wearing a vest."

She made an "ah" noise and pointed to the man.

"Well, our John Doe decidedly was not. You're the one who shot him, I'm guessing?"

Foster nodded.

He felt no joy or pride in taking a man's life, but he was confident that he'd made the right call. Especially after a search of his belongings showed plastic zip ties, a knife and a baggie of white pills in his deep pockets. The pills were being examined at the moment, but the zip ties alone had shown concerning intentions that the man had been harboring for Millie.

"Was that all you did?" Dr. Alvarez added. "Shoot him, I mean. Did you physically lay hands on him at all or any other contact?"

Foster shook his head. "No, but he was struck with a lamp, a book and was thrown into a wall by a woman holding a bag of laundry."

Dr. Alvarez tilted her head a little at the information. She didn't seem satisfied with it.

"First of all, I would love to hear that story in more detail. Second, that might explain his busted lip but a bag of laundry definitely didn't do this."

She moved the sheet down, revealing Coveralls'

bare upper body. He'd been cleaned, but the bullet hole was still an angry red against his pale skin.

It wasn't the only thing.

Foster took a step closer and shook his head.

"Definitely not a lamp or book either."

Coveralls' torso had a smattering of black, blue and purple bruises across it. He looked like he'd been someone's personal punching bag. Foster pointed to his upper arm where Millie had claimed to hit him with the bat to get away in the woods. The spot had also bruised.

"He was hit with a bat in self-defense last night, hours before the second attack. But only on the arm and only once. I have no idea about the rest of these bruises."

Dr. Alvarez reached out with her gloved hands and hovered above the main cluster.

"Okay, so the arm bruising and the busted lip fits that timeline," she said. "But *these*, these have already been healing."

"Which means Millie had nothing to do with them."

"Not likely. That's why I called you in." She shrugged. "I can't tell you why it happened or who or what did it yet, but I *can* confidently tell you that probably around two days ago this man took one heck of a beating."

THE HEAT OF midday warmed the back of Millie's shirt and exercise pants. She was tired, hungry and nervous all at once, standing there in front of the door to her home.

She wanted to go inside and, at the same time, she wanted to do anything but.

If Detective Lovett hadn't been with her, she might have gone to work despite her boss telling her to take the day off. She might have also said yes to Larissa's offer of taking refuge at her home. She might have just stood there, staring on the front porch.

Frozen.

But the detective was there, and he'd already promised he wasn't leaving her just yet.

"I know you're probably ready to finally get some sleep, but I'd personally feel better if I could clear the house before I go to my own," he said. "If that's okay with you."

It was more than okay to Millie, but she didn't say it in that way. She didn't admit she'd been afraid and anxious just thinking about being alone in her house.

Instead, she unlocked the door and stepped aside to let him in.

"Thank you," she said to him as he passed.

He waved her off, his detective's badge around his neck swaying at the movement.

"It's the neighborly thing to do."

Millie stood in the entryway as Foster checked every room, window and lock. He looked good for a man running on no sleep, even better for a man who had been shot no less than a handful of hours ago.

Then again, he'd already managed to save her twice.

Twice on the same day that she'd dismissed him to his face.

Millie ran a hand across the back of her neck. Tendrils of exhaustion felt like they were coming up through the floorboards, wrapping around her body and pulling down.

That tug became more powerful when her gaze swept to the one spot she'd been hoping to avoid.

A man had died in her home.

Bled out in her living room.

Now the man was gone, but the blood that had seeped into the rug was still there.

A stain.

A reminder.

One that made her stomach tight and already-fried nerves almost painful. Her discomfort must have shown. When the detective came back into the room with an all clear, he pointedly looked at the rug.

"There's not a thing you can do to save it, I hate to say. No amount of carpet cleaner or stain remover is going to get it looking like new. But we can try if you want."

That surprised Millie. Not that the rug was ruined but the implication that he'd help her try to clean it.

She shook her head.

"Even if we could get it looking like new, I don't think I could ever *not* see him there when I looked."

Detective Lovett didn't fault her for the truth.

Instead, he surprised her again.

He took off his holster, his badge, rolled up his sleeves and picked up her coffee table like it was as light as a toothpick. He placed it on the bare hardwood floor next to the rug, then turned his sights on the couch.

"You don't have to do that," Millie said. "I can clean all this up."

He winced but shook his head.

"You've already seen a lot that you shouldn't have had to see. But me? I've been around things like this before. You deserve a break and I don't mind giving you one." The couch wasn't by any means a heavy item, but it was still impressive to watch the man push it out of the way like it too was weightless.

The detective might not have had muscles bulging through his clothes, but there was no denying that there was strength in him.

"Trash pickup doesn't come until Friday, but I can take care of it before then."

Millie watched as the man who had been told he had bruised ribs and a slight concussion by the ER doctor hours before single-handedly re-arranged her living-room furniture, rolled up a bloodstained rug and then dragged it outside and into the bed of his pickup in the driveway next to hers. All without complaining one single bit.

His act of kindness, more than realizing he'd taken a bullet meant for her, did something to Millie.

When he came back in and asked where her floor cleaner was and then shooed her while he went back to the spot and cleaned it, that something turned into something more.

Despite that something, though, Millie couldn't help but ask the one question that had embedded itself in the back of her mind the moment the man in coveralls had appeared in the hallway.

"Do you think Fallon disappearing was because of that man? Or do you think I'm lying for my brother?"

They were back out on the front porch, the sun shining against the wet grass in front of them, the house smelling of Lysol behind them.

Detective Lovett's green, green eyes met hers.

He didn't look away as he answered.

"I don't think for one bit that you're lying, Miss Dean. Just like I don't think your brother left town for attention." He smiled. It was brief but helped her all the same. "And I'm going to do my damnedest to prove both."

That was it.

That was enough.

Millie closed the space between them with an embrace she hadn't expected to give.

The man was hard and warm against her body. His hands were soft, though, as one skimmed across her back.

"Thank you, Detective," she said into his shoulder. "Thank you."

She couldn't see his expression when he responded, but his tone was different. She just didn't know why.

And she didn't care.

Not right then.

Not when someone finally believed her.

His words rumbled from his chest into hers, melting away the layer of anxiety that had built up in the last day.

"Call me Foster."

Chapter Seven

Rosewater Inn had been a tragic attempt at a bed-and-breakfast in Kelby Creek's early 2000s. Converted from a somewhat nice-looking motel into a fancier-looking motel, it had missed every mark on trying to be unique and charming. The inn had gone broke faster than Foster and Regina had when they'd first moved out to Seattle.

However, after they'd left Kelby Creek behind, the inn had been repurposed again, achieving the unique descriptor with the additional one of just plain weird.

Or, as Foster's mother would have said, *eclectic*.

The one-story rooms that stretched to the west and included the lobby had been gutted and turned into a bar. The rooms that stretched toward the east had kept their interior walls and been made into micro-office spaces. Only one was currently rented out to a Mrs. Zamboni, a palm reader whose real name was Helen Mercer. It was an upgrade from her previous spot in her parents' basement, that was for sure. The last of the rooms, set dead center in front of the long parking lot, still had the remains of the fancier version of the motel locked inside their rooms.

Foster spotted a bare box spring mattress and dust-covered wooden end tables as he peeked through the opening in a curtain covering the window of room 4A. He was surprised when a woman cleared her throat next to him.

Mrs. Zamboni herself was giving him a grin. Foster had to make sure he didn't stare too long at the crown of flowers she had woven into her dyed-silver hair or her very pregnant stomach. He knew from experience that commenting on either would earn him a one-way trip to confrontation town.

So, Foster went the safe, neutral route instead. He stood tall again and pulled a smile on. Not that smiling at his former sister-in-law ever put any points in his favor in her book.

"Hey, Helen, how are you?"

Helen rubbed a hand over her stomach and gave him a look that was all annoyance.

"I'm eight months pregnant during the beginning of an Alabama summer and my last client asked me if I could talk to the dead so he could apologize to his neighbor for being awful to his dog." She motioned to him with a wave of her hand. "Then on my way to get some snacks that I really don't need, I run into the son of a biscuit who took my sister away from her family and didn't even have the decency to bring her back when he was done with her."

Helen, all five feet of her, had always had a tendency to run hotheaded. She was two years younger than Regina and the most outspoken of the Becker clan.

Which meant she'd commented on every single milestone of Foster and Regina's relationship, most vocally their divorce.

Foster sighed, knowing there was no right response to avoid a talking-to from the woman.

The moment he saw the Mrs. Zamboni, Palm Reader, sign, he should have bolted.

"I had no say or right to tell Regina what to do after the papers were finalized. She's the one who chose to stay in Seattle with her new boyfriend. Talk to her if you're mad about it."

Helen snorted. Foster was immediately reminded of Deputy Park. He'd been acting like a disgruntled employee for the last three days. Helen looked like she was the one who wanted to complain to the boss now as she continued speaking.

"You know, when she said you were coming back, we didn't believe it. Dad said you'd have a lot of nerve to show back up anywhere within the county lines." She rubbed her pregnant belly again and smiled. "I guess I'm going to have some fun facts for him at family dinner tonight."

Foster wasn't an idiot. He knew a major drawback of coming home again would be largely attached to his former family-in-law but hope sprung eternal that he'd at least avoid the bulk of them for a while.

At least until he was settled in.

"You only get one hometown, so I thought why not come back and try to help mine," he said. "It's as simple as that."

Helen's demeanor shifted from annoyance to genuine interest as her eyes went down to the badge hanging around his neck. It was clear she'd forgotten his profession.

And now she was curious as to why he was there during the workday.

"Are you looking for someone?"

Foster shrugged. "More like getting reacquainted with the local haunts." It was a lie and a truth. Foster needed to do what he said but he was also looking for gossip on a particular person. Or the person in question himself.

William Reiner. A potentially angry man whose career had been ended by Fallon Dean.

Foster readjusted his stance and tried to look nonchalant.

Helen's eyebrow rose with her obvious suspicion of him.

"Does that have anything to do with what happened over on Lively Drive Monday night?"

Her eyes widened. "Wait. Were you the one who killed the home intruder?"

Foster couldn't help it; he took a jab.

"Aren't you supposed to be psychic, Helen? Shouldn't you already know?"

She rolled her eyes so hard Foster bet she came close to permanent damage.

"I read *palms*. I'm not a one-stop shop to everything psychic, so you can put that one back in your holster and shut it. But I'm guessing it was you since you didn't give me a straight answer."

"I can't talk about an ongoing investigation. You know that."

Helen didn't look impressed.

"This town is a fishbowl," she said with a shrug. "The truth will come back around whether you say a word about it or not."

Foster knew that to be true.

Which was why he'd had a stern conversation with almost half of the sheriff's department to make sure everyone was on the same page about *not* sharing information outside of themselves.

"Then you'll hear about it later." Foster wanted to end the conversation there but, despite his feelings about Helen, she'd grown up and grown older in Kelby Creek.

She knew its people more than most.

"Speaking of fish in this fishbowl, do you know William Reiner?"

Helen was faster to speak her mind than hide what she was thinking. She made a face.

"We're not social but I know of him. He used to work at the sheriff's department. He lost his little brother to The Flood."

That was news to Foster.

"How was the brother involved?"

"According to officials, he wasn't. According to the rest of town? Well, he sure seemed guilty of something. He up and left during the FBI's investigation. Put his badge and gun on his desk and ran."

Foster took his notepad out of his pocket and clicked his pen to ready.

"What's his name? Reiner's bother."

"Cole but, like I said, as far as I've heard he wasn't found guilty of anything."

"But you said he ran?"

Helen nodded. "He sure didn't take his time in leaving."

"Do you know if Reiner ever explained why?"

Helen sighed. "No, but, based on the fact that he came to me asking questions like I was some kind of crystal ball, I'm guessing he didn't know either."

Foster hadn't expected that either. What he knew of Deputy Reiner, which was mostly from his work files, was that he seemed to be a no-nonsense man. One who wouldn't go to a psychic or palm reader, let alone believe in them.

"And what exactly did he ask?"

Helen shook her head. "That charm might have worked with my sister, but you're not getting anything about my clients from me, Detective. I respect their privacy." She took a step out into the parking lot, hand doing a lap over her stomach again. "If you have questions for Reiner, then you've come to the right place. He's a regular at Rosewater Bar." Foster watched after her, his annoyance waning at the encounter. It seemed like everyone in Kelby Creek had to deal with the past, one way or the other.

Foster's phone vibrated in his pocket before he could leave his spot in front of the old motel.

It was Deputy Park and he got straight to the point.

"We found something."

MILLIE ANSWERED THE door with a crown of curls, a denim skirt and a blouse that dipped low and clung tight. Her sandals were flat, but her toenails matched the manicure that Larissa had given her after their shift at the store that morning. Millie had also gone bold with her makeup. Dark red lipstick that looked almost violet in certain lights complemented eyeshadow that told the general public this was an intentional outing, and not a spur of the moment one.

Though seeing a certain blond standing on her

welcome mat didn't bode well for her evening plans when she opened the door.

"Detective?"

Foster had his badge around his neck and wasn't smooth in the least as he looked her up and down.

But he did catch himself.

"Hey, Millie, uh, sorry, did I catch you at a bad time?"

The heat of a blush was immediate. It ran up from her stomach and to her neck, promising to show the man that she was embarrassed.

Embarrassed that she'd been caught.

She laughed lightly, stalling.

If he knew about her plan, then he would probably point out it was at best useless, at worst a deeper hole that she'd find herself in.

If he *didn't* know about her bad plan, then there was no way anyone could trace any blame back to him for knowing about it before it was executed.

The devil on Millie's shoulder cheered at the thought of sidestepping the truth as a courtesy, yet the angel on the other told her to stare into the man's eyes.

Vibrant. Searching. The windows into the soul of the man who had taken a life to save hers.

Millie caved all within the span of two seconds.

"I was about to leave, actually. I'm going out. To the bar."

"Oh."

Millie didn't know why she wanted to, but she decided to let him know it wasn't a social visit.

"Alone," she blurted out. That blush found her cheeks and burned. She tried to be less awkward but sighed in defeat. "In all honesty, I'm hoping I can run into William Reiner and get him to talk to me."

In the last three days, Millie had seen Foster a total of two times. The first encounter had been the day after he'd taken the bloody rug from her house and promised her answers on the front porch. He'd been in full-blown work mode with a pad of paper in hand and a voice that sounded like a rehearsed recording. He'd broken down what he'd learned about the man who had come into her home after Fallon.

His name was Jason Talbot, according to his dental records, and Millie had never met or heard of him before seeing him in the woods. Past that, they had still been running down information on the, according to Foster, "surprisingly slippery" suspect. As for the pills that had been in Jason's pocket, those had been identified as a black-market off-brand of Paxil, an anxiety and depression medication.

"These popped up in a case I had in Seattle a few years back," he'd said. "Not the most common or popular of drug on the market, so we might be able to actually track them to the seller and see if we can get more information on Talbot."

He'd told her that was one of several new leads the department was working on.

"If we find out why Jason wanted Fallon in the first place, that can only help us get closer to what happened to Fallon," he'd added when Millie must have made a face. "We follow Jason, we also might find out who the woman in the woods is. Because so far no one in this county or the next has reported anyone missing or filed any reports of something similar happening. So, Jason is our goal right now."

The second time Foster had come over had been the day after that. It was less of an update and more of a checking-in.

"It's not an easy thing, being attacked. Same with seeing a body," he'd said, standing on her front porch with his badge yet again. "I just wanted to let you know if you need me you can call anytime."

Millie had been running late for work then. Had she not, she might have asked him inside. For what, she wasn't sure, but the urge had been there.

Just like it was with him there on her porch for the third time.

Foster had been a hard man to read the last two visits, but now, it was clear she'd surprised him.

He tilted his head to the side a little, eyebrows furrowing together.

"Why do you want to talk to Reiner?"

"I don't *want* to talk to the deputy, but, well, I was thinking about it and if Fallon did have one true enemy in town—someone who had a good reason to have it out for him—it would be Reiner. So I thought I'd see if he wouldn't mind casually talking to me about what he was up to six months ago..."

Suddenly Millie felt like a silly child.

If Foster felt the same way, he didn't say it. Instead, his forehead creased again in thought.

"You've never asked him before about Fallon's disappearance?"

Millie shook her head.

"Detective Gordon interviewed him, but other than him saying, 'He isn't involved,' I never got any explanations. Fallon and I hadn't talked to William Reiner or his family since he was forced to retire. And even then it was more of his wife yelling at Fallon while Reiner gave us the stink eye." She sighed. "It's been an unwritten rule of this town since then that the Deans give all Reiners an extremely wide berth."

"But now you think he might be involved."

Millie gave him the half-hearted shrug of a frustrated sister.

"Honestly, it's like I'm going out into the woods again looking for hope where there is none. I have no idea if Reiner had anything to do with Fallon disappearing, but he's one of the only stones I personally haven't overturned. So, I thought 'why not?'"

Foster was quiet a moment.

Thoughtful?

Trying to find a way to tell her not to go?

Regretting his move back to Kelby Creek and into the house next to hers?

Millie hoped the latter wasn't true.

Though she couldn't blame him if it was.

In less than a week he'd come to her rescue twice, been shot and had to shoot someone else.

That would definitely be grounds for a solid helping of regret.

However, instead of shaking his head at her, Foster's contemplation turned excited.

He nodded. "That's not a bad idea, actually." He flipped his wrist over to show his watch. It looked expensive, but the leather band was worn. "It's after five so I'm technically off the clock. Unless there's an emergency, of course. Do you mind giving me a few minutes to change?"

Millie felt her eyebrow rise. Just like a fluttering in her stomach.

"To change?"

"Yeah. So I can come with you. Actually, if you want I can drive too. I don't mind." He was already backing up, mind seemingly already forming a plan she wasn't privy to yet. "Meet you at my truck in five?"

"Uh, yeah. That works."

The words came out before Millie realized she'd said them.

Then the detective was off the porch and hurrying to his own next door.

Chapter Eight

If Millie had known how the night would end, she would have stayed home. In fact, she would have not only stayed right there in her house, but she would have told Foster to join her.

To stay a while together, doors locked and the world firmly outside.

But Millie had no idea that her simple bad plan would be the start of a night that she hoped to simply survive.

Hindsight was twenty-twenty, and when Foster jogged back out to his truck, looking roguishly handsome with his black tee, Wrangler jeans and tousled golden hair that fell against his shoulders as he ran a hand through it, the only thought in Millie's head was to ignore how her body said, "yes, ma'am, don't mind if I do" at the sight.

Foster Lovett was a good-looking man even when he wasn't saving her life.

"You're not going to wear your badge?" Millie mentally cringed. Her words went up an octave like she was some schoolgirl nursing a crush.

The detective made her nervous. She cleared her throat and tried again. "I mean, you know, if you need to ask questions in an official capacity."

Foster shifted the blazer he had draped over his arm. She could see his holster, gun, and badge on a chain beneath it.

"I'll bring them just in case, but I've found from experience that people are a lot chattier before you show them the badge."

He opened the passenger's side door and held his hand out to help her in. The skin-to-skin contact didn't help Millie's newly flared nerves. She hadn't intended to spend her time at the bar as a part of a twosome.

"So, do *you* think Reiner has something to do with Fallon?" she asked when he was seated behind the wheel. "I mean is that why you wanted to come along?"

Foster twisted around to put his blazer and gun in the back seat. Millie caught a whiff of a deep and delicious cologne coming off him.

She tried to rein in her senses and focus on his answer only.

"A lot of the older files at the department aren't exactly up to my standards," he said, careful as he chose his words. "That includes Fallon and Deputy Reiner's incident five years ago. So I wouldn't mind asking a few of my own questions. Plus it's been a long while since I've been back to Kelby

Creek. I've never actually been inside Rosewater as a bar, and I'm curious as hell."

He gave her a grin and turned over the engine. It fussed a little showing its age, but Millie liked the sound. Growing up, her father had been a big fan of older trucks. It was the reason why Fallon had his 1979 Chevy pickup with its light dusting of rust across the bumper instead of something more modern. She suspected it was his attempt at staying connected to a father he had truly loved.

"You know, I have to admit that I didn't realize you'd lived in Kelby Creek before now," she said. "My friend Larissa said you even grew up here?"

Foster laughed, taking them out to the street and pointing the vehicle toward the neighborhood exit. For a famed detective he seemed oddly at ease and not at all as uptight as Millie would have expected. He seemed like a man you'd want to get a beer with instead of a man who went after criminals and worse.

"I did. Born and raised in a house not even ten minutes from here."

"So you have family here?"

He shook his head. "I used to, but after my dad passed a few years ago my mom moved to Huntsville to live with her best friend." He laughed again. Even in profile his smile was easy on the eyes. "I've *almost* gotten used to getting random drunk calls from them when they've had a little too much wine while watching one reality show or another. It's a special kind of awkward to be at a murder scene and have your mom call you upset that Bachelor Mark, or whoever, picked the wrong woman."

Millie couldn't help but join in with a laugh. Just like she couldn't help imagining the man at a crime scene, notepad in hand, and eyebrows drawn together in deep concentration. For extra effect she imagined his long hair slicked back while the dreary Seattle sky sat as his backdrop.

"Kelby Creek sure has to be a far cry from Seattle."

Foster slowed to a stop at a light. Night was falling and the smell of rain had followed them into the cab of the truck. South Alabama summers only ever had two modes: hot and humid or humid and thunderstorms. Millie hoped no showers were headed their way. The only thing she'd grabbed before leaving her house was a small purse. She could picture her umbrella perfectly in a holder by the door.

"I was eighteen when we first got out to Seattle. Life happened fast there, really fast, for two South Alabama teenagers who'd never been out of the state until then. We got swept up in that pace for a few years. School. Work. More Work. Repeat. I grew a lot, changed a lot, and when we got used to the pace, I realized two things." He ticked off both points on his fingers as he said them. "One, I love being a detective and, despite all of the bad things I've seen, I'd make the same career choice in a heartbeat." Millie heard his mood shift in his tone. Anger. "And, two, even though I left Kelby Creek in my rearview as fast as lightning, I still am extremely protective of it."

"The Flood," she guessed.

He nodded. "I had just wrapped up a particularly nasty homicide and the local paper covered the story. It went from stating the facts about what had happened to my victim's poor family and closing the case for them to how miraculous it was that someone from Kelby Creek could be in law enforcement and not be dirty."

"Ouch."

"Yeah. After that something just clicked for me," he continued. "I reached out to Sheriff Chamblin and said I wanted to help in the rebuild. A week later I had the job."

Millie wanted to say that was noble of the man, but something he said had her stuck so she looped back.

"You said *we* moved to Seattle? Did that person also come back with you?" Millie felt that blush again. She hurried to sound less like a curious teenager and more like a considerate neighbor. "I just mean I've only seen you come and go from the house."

Foster snorted as he turned on the street where Rosewater was located.

"My high school girlfriend and I eloped the

second we were both eighteen. It wasn't until we both hit twenty-eight that we finally admitted that was a mistake. We're a whole lot better as friends now. I just wished we'd realized that sooner."

Out of her periphery Millie saw him turn his head to look at her. She didn't rightly know how to react. A part of her felt an unreasonable amount of jealousy surge at the idea of him being married for ten years while the other part of her was cheered at the fact that he was *no longer* married.

Then she thought of Fallon and Jason Talbot and William Reiner.

It was sobering.

"Well, I'll be honest. I'm glad you're here now."

Millie met his eyes. He gave her a small smile, but neither said anything until they were parked in the Rosewater lot.

Foster was all focus. He was already scanning the cars around them, no doubt trying to take in all the details.

Millie should have been too, but what he said next only made the bundle of nerves within her multiply.

"If Reiner is in there, let's not bombard him as soon as we're through the door. Let's treat this like a date and get our own table and drinks first. Then we can go from there. I don't want to spook anyone."

Millie's concentration shattered on the word

date. It didn't have a chance to recover before Foster was retrieving his blazer.

"Sounds good," she agreed out loud.

Yet inside she was struggling.

Pretend it's a date, Millie. No big deal, the angel on her shoulder told her.

Whatever the devil had to say, Millie decided not to listen to it.

THE ROSEWATER BAR had been converted into one long and narrow room. The bar stuck out from one wall while the bathrooms had been tucked to one side at the back. The only door you could go into past those belonged to the kitchen, a straight shot from the former lobby's front doors. Most of the locals knew that through the kitchen was the office where Gavin Junior, current owner of all of Rosewater, did the mundane paperwork part of bar-owning while his bartender would occasionally use the space to smoke a joint.

Only a handful of people knew the secret that connected all three of the spaces.

He moved along the two-by-fours in the attic space above the bar with familiar precision. It wasn't his first time going high to listen to the chatter below, and it wouldn't be the last either.

That didn't mean he wasn't nervous when he walked above the heads of the patrons.

Once he'd misstepped and had seen what could

have happened in his mind like a slow-motion horror movie.

One wrong step and he could have very well fallen through the Sheetrock and landed in the laps of the people he'd been listening in on. That, no doubt, would have resulted in him landing somewhere else.

Jail.

Or worse.

It wasn't like Kelby Creek always stuck with following the law.

Another time he'd shuffled along the beams with too much enthusiasm, knocking loose a thin sheet of dust that had floated down onto a table of patrons. Then he'd had to stand still for almost an hour to make sure no more dislodged and drew attention up at him.

Wouldn't that have been a kick in the pants? Everything he'd been working toward, and some ceiling dust gave him and his secret away.

So that night he was careful as he moved along the beams. Methodical in practice, attentive to every single move.

Slow and steady doesn't win any race. Careful and confident does.

He replayed this mantra over and over in his head until he was at one of the two vents that hadn't yet been closed since the renovation. They served no other purpose other than being a grated window that looked down into the bar.

Slowly he knelt, making sure no body part was in danger of slipping off a beam, and surveyed that night's crowd, hoping tonight was finally the night.

To say what he saw surprised him was an understatement.

Or, rather, *who* he saw.

Millie was seated at the most popular table along the right wall, situated beneath a neon sign that spelled out Danger, High Voltage and across from a man he didn't recognize. She was wearing her party clothes and had one of Rosewater's Pink Drinks between her hands. From his vantage point he was looking diagonally down at her but could see the smile she was sporting for her date.

He sat there for a while, trying to hear what they were saying but Millie and her companion had the good sense to keep their voices low. Most nights he was lucky to get loud patrons who only became louder the more they drank.

Check the other vent.

The mental reminder, since time got lost between the rafters when he became distracted, made him abandon his attempt at eavesdropping. He was careful as he pushed up and walked over to the vent opposite.

This one gave him a better view of the front doors and the middle of the main room.

And William Reiner's usual seat.

Since his wife had left him, William had been

a constant at Rosewater. The same beer, the same small table and the same sour face. He never had another soul sitting across from him, and he never was interesting at all.

Tonight would be no exception, he decided.

Plus Millie was there.

And she'd never been there before.

That had to mean something, right?

He went back to the first vent, deciding to put his attention there for the night, but came up short when the table showed empty. He bent lower and tried to see the rest of the room.

Where had they gone?

Like a mouse caught in a maze, he scuttled back over to his only other view into the bar. Millie and her date were probably leaving, though they hadn't been there long. Still, Millie Dean had never been known to spend a lot of time in bars.

Maybe they were going to a late movie or—

"Well, I'll be..."

Millie and the man weren't headed for the front doors but had instead gone straight to another patron's table.

William Reiner's to be specific.

That couldn't be good.

Not after Jason's death.

He pulled out his phone, triple checked that the flash on his camera was turned off, and took the best picture he could through the grates. It wasn't as flattering an angle of Millie but it put her and her date side by side, something he knew would be interesting to his boss.

He tried to stay a while to listen but even with the addition of William the group's volume remained low.

Whatever they were talking about couldn't be heard.

Which made him nervous, and he bet he wasn't the only one.

Chapter Nine

Millie opened her eyes. Pain hit her faster than clarity. The groan that left her mouth was instinctual; rolling over and finding a bucket in time for her Pink Drink to come back up was luck.

If she hadn't been so disoriented *and* in the process of emptying her stomach, she might have felt fear radiate up her spine as a hand touched her back. Instead, all she could focus on was the relief that came after a smooth, deep baritone spoke.

"You're okay. You're okay."

Foster.

It was Foster.

Whatever was going on, it felt nice to know that he was there with her.

But where *was there*?

He shifted behind her, but his hand didn't stop stroking her back until she was done getting sick. Millie would have normally been embarrassed, but confusion, pain and fear had put every normal reaction on the back burner.

She wiped her mouth on the back of her hand and

shook her head. The pain that had made her sick swam from the top of her head to behind her eyes.

She didn't understand.

What had happened?

Why had she woken up when she didn't remember ever falling asleep?

Millie let herself be turned back over. Foster helped her to sit up. Her head was foggy. Slushy. Not able to put the clues from around them together to create a picture that made sense. A dim light was coming from a flashlight just beyond her feet on the floor. The light showed a small, small room around them. Not at all what Millie had expected.

Not that she expected anything.

"Wh-what's going on?" she asked, voice hoarse. "Where are we?"

The room was the size of a small bathroom or maybe a large closet. Metal walls had peeling and bubbled-up paint. The floor was cold and in the same poor condition as the walls. Old linoleum squares came up in places, bare in others. An opened box was turned over and empty just beyond the flashlight. A mop was against the wall next to a small window that had been spray-painted black. Then there was the bucket next to her.

That was it.

There was nothing else in the room other than them.

"Are you okay?" Foster didn't answer her question but, based on the blood across his face and his torn shirt, he might not have known how.

He took her face in his hands. It was a gentle movement that Millie appreciated, considering how she felt.

"I—I don't know. My head feels cottony? And it hurts."

"What about the rest of you? Anything else?"

Millie did a quick mental scan of her body.

"Everything else feels normal. What about you? You're bleeding."

He didn't let her face go as Millie reached out and lightly touched his cheek, beneath the blood. For the moment it was just the two of them touching, trying to make sense of something.

"My head also feels off but I'm fine." He ran his thumb across her cheek and let her go, only to then pause his hand in midair. "I definitely fought someone."

He titled his hand so she could see his knuckles. They were busted and bloody.

"I don't understand. *What happened?* The last thing I remembered was being at Rosewater."

It was like someone had rubbed the memory right out of Millie's head. One second she was drinking a Rosewater special drink and coming up with a plan to talk to William Reiner, and the next moment was just gone.

"I think we were drugged." Foster stood with

a slight wobble. "I can't remember anything past walking up to Reiner in the bar."

Well, that was more alarming than Millie had expected.

"Drugged? As in things they do in the movies?"

Foster nodded as he walked the few steps over to the mop. Then he was back at her side, reaching down to help her stand.

"It would explain the gaps in memory and how our heads feel," he said. "I'm thinking someone could have spiked our drinks."

Millie was less of a wobble on her feet and more of a stumble. Foster wrapped his arm around her and turned them both around to face the only door in the room.

It was narrow and old, sitting at the top of two stairs. Two *plastic* stairs. The room didn't make sense, not that anything else did, but the feeling of queasiness that was still in the pit of Millie's stomach was familiar.

She didn't place it until Foster had her positioned behind him with the mop handle as her weapon and him with the small flashlight about to try to open the door.

"Foster. I think we're on a boat."

As soon as she said it, Millie knew it was true. The room wasn't a room. It was a cabin. Not only were they on a boat, she was as sure as her motion sickness could be that they were also on the water.

Foster accepted that line of thinking with an even more severe frown.

"The creek is only wide enough for a boat this big at, maybe, three spots. All of those are a good twenty to thirty miles away from anything useful." He shook his head. "It doesn't make sense why we're *here* and not bound or with a captor watching us."

For the first time since gaining consciousness, Millie realized Foster's blazer, gun and badge were nowhere to be seen. Which meant whoever had done this to them could be armed with something that had been meant to protect them.

Foster must have seen the new flare-up of worry.

He closed the space between them and leaned his head down. His forehead touched hers. Warm and reassuring. She could even still smell his cologne. With one hand he held her arm, with the other he motioned to the mop handle. His words came out crystal clear.

"If you need to use this on anyone, when you swing don't imagine hitting them, imagine going *through* them. Okay?"

Millie nodded. It hurt.

Foster's face softened, but he didn't say anything more. He turned back to the door. Millie readied the mop handle like a baseball bat.

She held her breath as Foster tried the door.

It was unlocked. He slid it open slowly but with ease.

Millie tightened her grip on the mop handle, sure someone would be waiting.

Yet, the only thing that came for them was the ambient glow of darkness.

And water.

Millie had been right.

They were on a boat.

A boat that, aside from them, was empty. It was also in the middle of the water. Foster shone the light along a bank and its tree line to their right and then to another bank with more trees to their left. Millie could make out the dark water ahead of them and behind.

"We're anchored," Foster finally said. He turned his attention to a chain off the side of the boat. Millie went to the captain's chair and looked at the engine.

Since she had to have Dramamine in her system to even think about being on a boat, she wasn't that familiar with their intricacies. Still, it was easy to see the key to the ignition was gone. She said as much, and the two of them lapsed into a confused silence. Foster inspected every nook and cranny while Millie tried not to get sick again.

When he seemed to be done, she asked a few of the several questions she was holding on to.

"Why would someone anchor us here? In the middle of the creek, at night, and alone?"

Foster shook his head then shone his light to the tree line to their left. The bank had more sand than the one opposite it.

"One time I got called to the scene of a homicide while I was off duty. It was pouring rain and I got drenched." Millie felt her eyebrow raise at the subject change but then he pointed to his shoes. "I was wearing these, and it took almost a full day for them to completely dry out." He ran his hand along the closest part of the boat to him. Millie realized belatedly that it was wet. It had rained. "They're dry now, which means we were inside when it rained. That might help us with a timeline later."

"I guess it also means we never were *in* the creek," she added. "So does that mean that someone either drove us here and left us or used another boat to get us to this one, which was already anchored?"

Foster shook his head again. Millie wished there was better light for her to see him. His expression now looked haunted, shadows across his features that pulled at her. She went to him, so close that she could smell that cologne again.

"What do we do now?"

Foster moved the beam of light back to the bank.

"We swim for it, go find help, and then bring the entire sheriff's department back out here to tear this boat apart to look for any forensic evidence."

Millie looked out at the dark water.

The motion sickness part of her loved that plan.

The terrified-of-water-she-couldn't-see-through-never-mind-at-night part of Millie got a little weak in the knees.

Foster must have recognized the shift in her.

He surprised her, a feat considering their current situation, and took her hand in his.

"I'll be right next to you the entire time."

Millie would have been lying had she said that didn't make her feel better.

She nodded and winced at the pain.

"If there used to be a ladder here, it's not on board anymore," he said. "Even with the flashlight I can't see the bottom, so I'm going to try to lower myself over so we can figure out how deep it is before you jump in."

"Would it be too much to hope that it's shallow?"

The dark water was a nightmare and a half, waiting with menacing calm.

"Based on the fact there's an anchor, I'm assuming it's at least six feet. I just don't want to take our chances and jump in and break our legs."

Millie conceded to that, even if she wasn't a fan.

He squeezed her hand and then let go.

"That's only about thirty seconds of swimming from here to the bank. We can do this."

Millie knew the pep talk was for her, so she gave him a smile to let him know it landed. In the dim light they had to work with, Foster's green eyes still penetrated with ease. She felt a pang of disappointment when they left her to focus on the task at hand.

The flashlight was passed over to Millie as the detective perched on the side of the boat and then swung his legs over. With an impressive amount of upper body strength, he used his arms to lower himself until he was no longer moving himself down but holding on. Millie leaned over and watched him let go.

The darkness went up to his shoulders before he started treading water.

"Can you touch the bottom?" Millie asked with hope clear in her voice.

He dipped down, the water going to his chin, before popping back up.

"No dice. Whoever picked this spot knew it was deep."

Millie's fear response might not have liked it but her stomach was reminding her that she needed to get to land sooner rather than later. She passed the flashlight down to Foster and finally let go of the mop.

She had never been the fastest swimmer, but she was pretty sure she was about to temporarily acquire Olympic-level speed as soon as she hit the water.

Knowing she couldn't do the cool, strong man way of getting in like Foster had, Millie sat on the edge and threw her legs over until she was sitting. Foster stayed close as she did a little hop off.

The water was surprisingly warm. Foster reached out to try to keep her above the water, but Millie's spaz level at being in the dark water made her move more than she meant to. Her head went under in an instant.

It felt like a second went by.

Just one.

Yet it was enough time to take their already tilted world and turn it upside down.

FOSTER WASN'T A MAN to believe in luck, good or not. It was an old fight he'd had with his ex-wife, Regina, from age fifteen when she had called him lucky to land a girlfriend like her to the day they signed the divorce papers and she cited their marriage had ended because of bad luck.

Good, bad, or anything in between, luck was just what you called the timing of something based on the outcome.

It wasn't good luck that Jason Talbot had found Millie alone in her home when he'd gone to question her about Fallon, just as it wasn't bad luck that he'd shown up minutes before Foster had.

Luck was the ripple effect of actions. Consequences of actions, whether accidental or intentional.

However, in the dark creek water, next to an abandoned boat he'd woken up on—after most likely being drugged—and treading next to a beautiful woman who had just resurfaced, Foster's disbelief in luck sank to the bottom.

Actual, physical ripples spread across the top of the water, diverting around Millie as she took a breath.

The ripples weren't coming *from* her but toward her.

Foster clicked off the flashlight.

Millie made a noise but something else farther off was louder.

Foster propelled himself backward in the water. Instead of turning toward the bank, he looked around the front end of the boat where the creek remained wide and snaked out of view around a bend of trees.

The fleeting existential crisis of bad and good luck warred within him as he moved back to Millie, careful not to move too much.

Millie's eyes were wide.

She'd heard it too.

It was good luck that Millie had gone overboard with as little sound as she had.

It was bad luck that they hadn't left for the woods sooner.

"A boat," he whispered, water lapping in his mouth while he took Millie's body in his arms and pulled her along with him. "We need to hide."

Chapter Ten

The second boat had at least two passengers.

Foster could hear their footfalls as they stepped onto the plastic flooring overhead. They'd docked their boat alongside the craft Foster and Millie had woken up on.

Had they come back for Foster and Millie?

Why had they left them in the first place?

There were too many questions and, while Foster was quick to let everyone know he loved a challenge, this wasn't what he'd meant.

One set of footsteps came closer to their side of the boat. Foster felt Millie's entire body tense against him. He probably wasn't faring much better. His muscles were all working toward two purposes. To keep Millie against the side of the boat as best he could and to be ready if their hiding place was spotted. Though he wished he could tell her with confidence that everything would be okay.

That this was all just some weird misunderstanding. That help was on its way and everything would be fine.

But he couldn't.

They were in a wild, unpredictable situation.

One he couldn't have imagined had he sat down at his desk and been told to try.

So if he couldn't promise her a good ending, he was going to make sure she knew he was going to fight for it at the very least. That included keeping her safe.

He pulled her against him with one hand so she didn't have to keep treading water and tightened his grip on a small, busted light protruding from the side of the boat.

However, even that play had its set of problems.

If the newcomers—whoever they were— looked out at the bank Foster and Millie had been about to make their way to, they would see nothing but water, sand and trees.

If they looked over the side of the boat and down, they'd see Foster and Millie trying to stay as still as possible in the deep, dark water.

Foster just hoped that they weren't that thorough. And that the other boat stayed on the opposite side of them.

"Be careful."

It was a man's voice, deep and with a thick Southern drawl that saturated the three short syllables. He was the one closer to them. Thankfully, he didn't seem too interested in inspecting further.

The other set of footsteps softened.

They'd gone down into the cabin.

It didn't take long for those same footsteps to come back topside.

"There's no one in there."

The second voice also belonged to a man. There was less twang to it. Foster also didn't recognize it.

"I don't believe it." The Southern drawl turned angry. His footsteps changed course as he must have gone to double-check his partner. He took a bit longer in his search and was none the happier when he was back outside.

"Someone got sick down there," he said matter-of-factly. "Which means *someone* was down there."

"Well, they sure ain't there now, are they?"

Foster stared into the warmth of Millie's eyes as the sound of a punch went through the night air. The receiver of the hit groaned. Foster's guess was it was the one who had less twang.

"You think this is all some kind of video game, don't you?" the Southern drawler said, voice raised so much that Foster didn't have to strain to hear him. "That every little damn hurdle we've hit is just a minor inconvenience. That all we have to do is go lay next to a beautiful woman and call it a day and everything resets in the morning."

There was movement again.

Foster wasn't sure but he bet it was another hit.

"This ain't a game, son. If it was, we'd be losing to a much better player." He muttered something, but it got lost in the distance between him and the water. Though Foster hazarded that it probably wasn't poetry.

A sigh broke the rant and seemed to help Southern Drawl calm himself down enough not to hit his partner again.

"That woman said she saw those two get muscled into the truck," he continued. "This is where he took Fallon, so this has to be where he'd have taken them."

Foster had dealt with the intersection of death and surprise for years during his career in Seattle. He'd been the one to notify a family member of their loved one's demise, and he'd been the one to take the confession of a killer in the interrogation room. Not every case was so cut-and-dried and not every one was about homicide, but from his time dealing with it all, Foster had picked up a skill that kicked into gear the moment Fallon's name had been said aloud.

It was knowing the gravity of the look on Millie's face at the mention of her brother.

That instinctual feeling a person had when something life-changing had been said. That piece of information or string of words that, once spoken, could never be unheard.

Millie had felt it.

And Foster knew the second she had.

Millie had a new lead to go on. An answer, just waiting for a question.

A question she was ready to ask, even if it meant putting herself in danger.

Foster leaned his head over so it pressed against her forehead.

No, he mouthed.

He wasn't sure if she saw it, but she kept quiet as the men kept talking.

"Someone puked down there so someone *was* here." This time it was the second man. The younger man, Foster decided. "He either came back for them or some drunk has been staying here and couldn't hold his liquor. Either way, what do you want us to do now?"

There was another sigh.

It deflated as fast as Foster heard the *third* boat.

The engine on it was in no way stealthy and sounded waterlogged and labored in the distance.

It also wasn't expected by the men above them. The younger one's voice split between obvious excitement and fear.

"Oh man, do you think it's him?"

The older man wasn't as thrilled. He also wasn't as loud.

Foster could hear that he was whispering but couldn't hear what he was saying.

Millie nudged his head with hers. He felt her shrug against him.

Even if they could talk, he didn't have answers for her.

Though that was going to change soon enough.

They waited as the men above them became quiet. Foster wasn't big on boats, but he knew enough to take a guess that the approaching one was much smaller than both crafts it was steering toward.

The person driving the boat stopped.

Ripples moved across the water.

Millie placed her hand against Foster's chest.

He didn't have to hear her to know she was thinking one thing.

Was Fallon the man on the other boat?

Or the man who had brought Fallon here before?

"Howdy there, guys."

Unlike the other two men, Foster recognized this voice in an instant.

Deputy Carlos Park.

"I was out looking for a buddy of mine and was wondering if you could help me?"

His voice echoed clearly around them. The same as Southern Drawl's.

"Well, howdy yourself, Deputy. We're just fishing, is all, I'm afraid. No one but us out here."

They knew the deputy?

Park asked exactly what Foster was wondering himself.

"I'm sorry but have we met before?" the deputy asked. "What's your name? The light on your boat isn't helping me get a clear view of you."

"Everybody in town knows who the law are," Southern Drawl replied. "You know, what with everything that's happened."

That took the conversation and made it stall. Deputy Park must have been trying to decide on what to do next. Foster wished he could see the men on the boat just like he wished he could see if they were armed.

Also, he might not have liked Deputy Park all that much, but he was a colleague. One who hadn't been found guilty or run during The Flood.

That should have counted for something.

And it did in Foster's book.

When the silence overhead saturated the air, fraught with tension he could feel all the way in the water, Foster made a few decisions of his own in rapid succession.

The first required the risk of making noise, but he had a feeling that group of men were focused on their conversation more than the water. He held his breath as he moved the hand he had around Millie and pushed her gently closer to the boat than him.

The ambient light of night had put a slight glow on the woman. Her eyes were still warm in the

shadows it created. They let him know in no uncertain terms that she understood what he was
trying to convey. Slowly she moved her hand up
to the busted light Foster was using as a hand-
hold. He kept her floating until she had a pur-
chase on it.

Then he let go of both her and the light.

The men on the boat had started talking about
their lie of fishing while, Foster suspected, Deputy Park was doing his own fishing for information. Or more time.

He could have been stalling, waiting for
backup.

Or he could see that one or both of the men
were armed and wasn't comfortable in a shoot-
out over the water.

Either way no one seemed to notice the lapping
of water as Foster came free of the boat.

Which was good because he needed some surprise on his side.

Stay. Here, he mouthed to Millie.

She nodded.

It was all the encouragement he needed.

Foster moved as quietly through the water as
he could, keeping his arms and legs beneath the
surface while propelling him to the back end of
the boat. Whatever light was on the strangers'
craft was enough to show Foster Deputy Park's
position.

And his body language. It might as well have

screamed that he was about to pull his gun even though he was alone. His hand hovered by his holster.

It was now or never.

Foster went to the busted engine. Its casing was cracked and crusted. The lip around it that led into the boat wasn't in the best of shape. The abandoned vessel was definitely a junker. Foster just hoped when he put his weight on the lip that it didn't break off completely. Trying to back up the deputy only to fall *back* into the water definitely wasn't ideal.

But could he get onto the boat without making any noise?

Absolutely not.

Would his sudden appearance cause him to draw fire from the deputy he was trying to help and the two potentially armed men?

Probably.

Foster did it anyway.

One second he was in the water and the next water was pouring off him and into the back of the boat.

The lip of the boat cracked before he was standing tall. Foster yelled out he was from the sheriff's department, but he wasn't about to stop to make sure they heard him correctly.

The two men who had boarded were standing a few feet apart. One glance in their direction showed both had guns. The man closer to Foster—the older one judging by the gray hair in a halo around his balding head—had a holster on his hip while his partner, a stout man with black hair and an outfit that looked like he was about to go golfing at the country club, had a shotgun down and resting against his leg.

Deputy Park *was* waiting for backup. Or, at least Foster assumed that was the case because as soon as the deputy saw him, he was the first to react. Which was good considering the younger man went for his shotgun like he aimed to use it. Foster couldn't let that happen.

He used his momentum to go for the older man, hoping to use him like Millie had used the bag of laundry against Jason Talbot, but his shoes couldn't get any traction. Foster stumbled into the older man and hit him at the knees. Instead of bowling over into his partner, they went down to the deck hard.

Then Foster did something on instinct.

He put absolute faith in Deputy Park. Instead of scrambling to get out of the way of the younger stranger's shotgun, Foster turned his attention to fighting the older man to keep his gun in his holster.

When the gunshot exploded through the air but Foster felt no pain, he realized he'd made the right choice.

The younger man toppled over. The shotgun hit the deck with a clatter, but Foster couldn't go for it yet. He had his hand fastened over the butt of the older man's gun and was actively punching him in the gut. Foster had to give it to the man, he was tough. He took each hit with a grunt before delivering his own.

The sound of water displacing synced with the older man landing a frustratingly accurate hit. His fist went into the section of bruised ribs that he'd gotten from Jason's bullet. While it mostly didn't hurt anymore while doing mundane tasks, getting hit square in those ribs by a man desperate for his gun made Foster roar in agony.

Which was probably why he didn't realize at first that Deputy Park *wasn't* the new arrival on deck.

Millie drove her fist down from the heavens with such quiet swiftness that neither Foster nor the older man saw it coming. For the rest of Foster's life, he doubted he'd ever see such a beautiful hit.

The older man recoiled from the force and, to everyone's surprise, he went limp.

Millie Dean had just knocked out a man with a sucker punch that was so precise that it could have taught its own class.

Foster wanted to praise her then and there, but he was hyperaware that they needed to get two guns away from the men.

"The shotgun," he breathed out, pain still radiating up his side.

Millie nodded, cradling her hand, and took possession of the discarded weapon as Foster pulled the handgun free of the older man's holster. She jumped back as the younger man groaned.

"Keep it on him but don't shoot," Foster directed her. He was slower to stand, but when he did, he was at her side, gun trained on the unconscious man just in case.

"Are you okay?" Millie asked, voice wobbling. Most likely from excess adrenaline.

Foster nodded. "What about you?"

"My hand hurts but I'm okay."

Foster snorted. "That was an amazing hit," he admitted. "Especially considering I told you to stay in the water."

Millie laughed. It too was a wobbling sound.

Someone cleared their throat.

Foster turned to see Deputy Park, gun hanging down at his side and mouth open like a fish trying to breathe out of the water.

He shook his head, eyes wide.

"What in the hell, y'all?"

Chapter Eleven

Millie was ready to leave the hospital, the doctor disagreed.

"You're in observation until I say otherwise," he'd told her with quite a stern look.

The tone, and look, had been deserved though, if she was being honest. Since they'd been brought to Haven Hospital, Millie had been ready to go to the department and question the man who had spoken about Fallon. Being drugged, losing almost eight hours of memory, and waking up sick after being dumped out in an abandoned boat thirty miles away from where they'd started at the bar?

Well, those details were irrelevant in Millie's opinion.

The man talking about Fallon was not.

Millie had been itching for the sheriff to change their course from the hospital to the department while driving her and Foster away from the dock where Deputy Park had sequestered the small boat. He'd been a steadfast *no* against forgoing a medical exam.

Foster had agreed with the man, though Millie could tell that the detective wanted to go and detect.

She could also tell that he was in pain.

He'd opted to sit in the back of the truck next to her, saying it was to save the sheriff's passenger's side seat from their wet clothes, but Millie suspected he was still trying to protect her.

Not that she minded one bit.

There might have been a lot of questions in the air around them, but there was one point of fact that was easy for her to admit.

She trusted Foster.

That was a rare thing for Millie, a phenomenon that wasn't lost on her.

Still, once they were at the hospital she tried her best to hurry the process of being examined, despite the detective telling her that they'd get the truth soon enough. The sheriff attempted to reassure her in private before they left.

"I've known that man in there since he was a baby," Sheriff Chamblin had said to her. "He's not the kind of person to let something go. Most times that's a great asset for a detective but, for a man who's just been beaten, drugged and shot all within the last week, it's not helping him." Sheriff Chamblin had taken off his cowboy hat with an acute look of concern. "I know you aren't a fan of the department and have a history with a lot of the town, but that man in there? He hasn't let you down an inch since you've met him. I'm pretty sure if you asked Love to go take on an army right now, he'd do it. Return the favor and make sure he gets the care and rest he needs to get better. In the meantime, I swear to you that we will do everything in our power to get to the bottom of this."

Millie would have taken offense at the implication that she was the one standing in the way of Foster's well-being, but the sheriff's words were heartfelt and genuine. So, she'd decided to calm down on her own.

"I'll make sure he listens to the doctor," she'd promised. "But, when we're out of here, y'all better not cut me out of this."

Sheriff Chamblin had put his cowboy hat back atop his head. Then he'd tipped it to her.

"Yes, ma'am."

After that, Millie had been a good patient, all the while keeping her impatience as quiet as possible. She'd given Foster space while the doctor saw to him in his room.

Now, a few hours later, Millie's resolve was breaking.

She peeked out of her room and into the hallway. A deputy named Lawrence was stationed down the hallway in the second-floor lobby. Foster had said they'd been assigned someone just in case another attack came their way. Yet Millie now saw that same man distracted by his phone. Had she not wanted to sneak into the detective's room, she might have been offended. She padded across the short space and was inside the room without a fuss.

It wasn't until she turned around and saw Foster standing at the foot of the hospital bed in nothing but his jeans that Millie realized she should have knocked.

She was also painfully aware of her less-than-flattering hospital gown.

"I—I should have knocked," she said in a stammer.

Millie intended to avert her eyes from his bare chest but, well, that's not what happened.

Not at all.

Millie already knew the detective was attractive. She'd already admitted that to herself, and she'd already had some stray, somewhat inappropriate carnal thoughts, but standing there, caught in a candid moment, Millie couldn't help but stare.

After they'd gotten to the hospital and been put into rooms, both had taken showers. Millie's makeup was gone, her hair was free and frizzy, and her right hand was scabbed and bandaged.

Foster, however, was a sight to behold.

His hair was dry now and waved to his shoulders, wild and golden even under the hospital fluorescents. The color matched the stubble along his jaw and the dusting of hair that went from his chest down to beneath his waistband. And that chest. Millie had felt the man's muscled body against hers in the water. Logically she knew how his body must have looked beneath his clothes.

Yet the lean muscles that went from biceps to abs gave her such great pause that, for a moment, she felt like she was caught in mental quicksand. Sinking lower and lower, in danger of getting completely lost.

Luckily, or not so much, it was the same bare skin that had her transfixed that pulled her out of her fascination.

"Oh my God."

Millie closed the distance between them with concern replacing appreciation in a flash. Her eyes locked in on his side.

"Is this where you were shot?"

It was unlike any bruise Millie had ever seen before. Dark and angry. Wide and unavoidable.

It looked absolutely painful.

Foster laughed. It was a light sound. It didn't feel right next to such ugliness.

"*And* where our friend Southern Drawl decided to hit me during our tussle. If I'd been a carnival game, he'd have walked away with an oversized stuffed monkey as a prize for hitting the bull's-eye."

He was trying to be funny about it, dismissive,

but seeing the horrible mark made Millie realize just how bad it would have been had Foster not been wearing his vest.

She reached out and felt his warm skin beneath her fingertips. She was careful, gentle.

"You could have died." Millie's voice had hollowed. For the first time since he'd disappeared, the worry for her brother was moved aside. "You could have died because of me, Foster. And not just once. The woods, Jason Talbot, Rosewater, the creek... You wouldn't have been in any of those situations if it weren't for me."

His hand was warm as it enveloped hers. Together they rested against his side. When he spoke, she could feel it through his body.

"You didn't pull the trigger, you didn't attack me and you didn't drug me and then dump me on a boat. Trust me. None of this was your fault."

"I'm the common denominator," she said simply. "And I'm so sorry."

Foster took his other hand and used it to angle her gaze to his. She noticed belatedly that he had a shirt in his grip. He could have been holding a flamethrower instead and she still would have kept her focus on his eyes.

"It's easy to blame yourself when you don't know who the real blame falls to." His smile was small. A whisper, almost. It brought her attention to his lips but not before being pulled right back up into those true green eyes. "And, by my count, you've been doing your fair share of having my back out there. Not many people I know, women or men, would take their chances at going against two armed men soaking wet. Never mind knocking one out cold with a picture-perfect punch. Who taught you how to hit like that anyway?"

Millie tried not to but she grinned.

"You did." Foster's eyebrow rose. "I just used what you told me to do with the mop. The whole 'imagine going through them' when you hit someone with a thing." She shrugged. "I figured it probably applied to humans too and not just mop handles."

Foster let go of her chin. His laugh lit up all of his features. Millie smiled along with him.

"Millie Dean, you are a surprise and a half. God sure broke the mold with you."

The warmth of a blush made its way to her cheeks.

"I don't know about that, but I'll take the compliment all the same." She cleared her throat as she pulled her hand away from the man. Then she took a small step back. She finally averted her eyes and motioned to the shirt he was holding. "Also, sorry I barged in here just now. I should have knocked. I didn't mean to catch you dressing. I guess I was starting to feel a little cramped…and a lot impatient just waiting around in bed."

Foster waved off her apology. Then he sighed.

"To be honest I was considering a jail break myself. Since I already got some sleep to make the doctor calm down, I figured I could get away with leaving."

"Oh?" Millie forgot to give the man privacy again. She snapped her head back toward him so quick, her hair shifted against her back. "Did you hear anything new?"

It was a generalized question, but she couldn't figure out which one to present first.

"I've been told that they found some new information but not what. Yet." He took his shirt and started to put it on. "So I figured I'd be harder to sidestep if I was in front of them."

Millie watched as he looped the T-shirt over his head and then paused before pulling it down.

He was stuck.

Millie reached out again, this time uncertain.

"Do you—"

"I've got it," he said, cutting her off with unmistakable male stubbornness.

Foster curled the shirt down to his shoulders. His face contorted as he paused again.

"Are you sure?"

He nodded. "I took a bullet to the vest and fought a man two days later. I think I can handle putting on a shirt."

Foster struggled on.

Millie held in a giggle.

When someone knocked on the door, the playfulness went away.

Millie took the bottom of his shirt in her hands and pulled down to cover his stomach. Foster didn't fight it.

"Come in," he called when his stomach was covered.

Millie put more space between them but didn't get too far. Their closeness was enough to draw a glance between them by the new arrival.

"Deputy Lawrence said I could come in."

The woman was a bouquet of color. From her patchwork blouse, red slacks, blue-striped hair and purple lipstick, she ate up the drabness of her surroundings with ease. It made Millie once again self-conscious of her gown and its garbage bag vibes.

"It's fine." Foster motioned between Millie and her. "Millie Dean, this is Dr. Amanda Alvarez, Dr. Alvarez, this is Millie Dean."

The doctor's height allowed her less than three strides before she was shaking Millie's hand.

"You can call me Amanda," she said, all smiles. "I'm the new Dawn County coroner."

"Oh! I read about you in the paper when you were hired," Millie said. "You're the youngest coroner in Kelby Creek history."

Amanda laughed. "That wasn't a hard feat considering I'm pretty sure the man I replaced had a personal relationship with the dinosaurs."

Millie had never met the former coroner but knew he was one of the many who had lost their jobs during The Flood. He'd been suspected of doctoring some of his reports in favor of keeping certain friends in places of power. Though, on the spot, Millie couldn't remember the specifics past that. Still, she laughed at the joke. A lot of the first round of people fired or incarcerated had been Kelby Creek's older, more prominent members.

"So what brings you out of the basement?" Foster swept his hand wide to the love seat next to the bed, offering her a seat. Amanda raised her hand to decline without saying the words.

"I'm actually here because your doctor has the hots for me." Foster shared a confused look with Millie. Amanda continued. "When he confirmed you two had been drugged with the same meds that had been found in Jason Talbot's possession the night he died, he came down to the basement and asked if Jason had had the same meds in his system. Unlike my predecessor, I told him I couldn't discuss the details about an ongoing investigation. And that seemed to be all I needed to say for *him* to start telling me about the details he knew."

Amanda took a step closer. On reflex Millie and Foster took a step in closer too. The doctor didn't lower her voice when she continued, but there was a quickness to her words. An excitement.

"Most of what he said, I had already heard through the grapevine of nurses and deputies hanging around when you were first brought in, *but* he told me something I wanted to make sure you knew. But first, can I see your hands?"

The question was to Foster. Again, he shared a look with Millie. Then he held up his hands. Amanda was quick to take them in hers to inspect.

"I heard you don't remember what happened between the bar and waking up on the boat, right?"

"Right."

"But your hands were busted like this when you regained consciousness but not when you first arrived at the bar."

Foster nodded. "Right again. Though I fought on the boat after."

Amanda poked one of Foster's knuckles. Some were still scabbed, some were still in the process due to his most recent fight. She looked thoughtful for a moment.

Then she nodded, seemingly to herself. She dropped his hands.

"I'm no detective and I certainly don't know the full extent of the case and what's going on right now—"

"But?"

Foster went from friendly to professional in an

instant. Millie couldn't blame him. He'd caught a scent.

Another piece of the puzzle.

Something that might lead them to the rest.

"You obviously hit someone," she said. "Hard enough to bust your knuckles. That suggests you either hit them so hard in one go that it broke the skin or, more likely, you dealt several blows."

"Yeah, I'm guessing I landed multiple hits. Why is that of interest?"

"Normally it wouldn't be, but from what I've heard? Neither of the men who were brought in with you this morning had any bruising or marks across their bodies other than the fresh hits."

Millie watched as realization dawned across Foster's face.

"What does that mean?" she asked, not quite there with him yet.

Amanda opened her mouth to answer, but Foster beat her to it.

"It means that whoever I fought during our missing gaps of memory definitely wasn't one of the men on the boat."

"If you have a suspect already, I'd also go see if they're sporting a new shiner," Amanda added. "Because I'm pretty sure a guy like you left a mark."

Millie's stomach went tight as she met Foster's gaze.

"The sheriff told us on the drive here that he

had already questioned William Reiner when we went missing," she said. "But did he say if Reiner had any bruising?"

Foster broke their huddle and went to the hospital phone next to the bed since their personal cell phones were still missing.

"No," he said, dialing a number. "But I'm sure about to ask."

Chapter Twelve

"And then she rose out of the water like Swamp Thing!"

Deputy Park sprung up from behind his desk and waved his hands at this audience in the sheriff department's bullpen for effect.

Foster cleared his throat.

Millie shifted at his side.

Deputy Park, however, didn't look like he'd been caught bad-mouthing the woman. If anything, he seemed excited to see them both. A distinct change from his past behaviors, that was for sure.

"Honestly, I've never seen anything so cool!" He was grinning from ear to ear. He addressed Millie directly. "I mean I had barely recovered from the detective here popping out of the water like a salmon going upstream, but then you rocked my world. It was some James Bond, spy-craft-type stuff if I ever did see it."

Foster smiled at Millie. Mostly because he agreed. He might not have seen the woman go through the motions, but he'd definitely benefited from her actions.

"I was just trying to help," she said shyly.

Deputy Park wasn't hiding his admiration.

"You didn't just help, you probably saved *someone*'s life out there."

Foster recognized the profound relief that flitted across the deputy's face as he put emphasis on "someone." It was brief but poignant. He wasn't spelling it out to Millie but, had she not helped, there was a good chance that Deputy Park would have had to take a kill shot had one of the men, or both, managed to take up their guns. Which meant there was a high chance that she'd saved him from his first causality in the line of duty.

Now Park was grateful, and Foster wasn't at all surprised by that.

"And if you hadn't shown up, things could have been a lot worse for us," Foster pointed out.

Park shrugged.

"If the Good Samaritan hadn't seen you two get taken and called it in, we wouldn't have known you were missing for a while," the deputy said.

"But you took that extra time they gave you, found tire tracks, and decided to check the water. That's good work. No matter which way you slice it." Park took the compliment with a smile. Foster followed it up with a question he was itching to ask. "Is the sheriff in his office?"

To say they all had questions was an understatement. Foster had been compiling and updating his own list of questions since he'd met Millie. The last twenty-four hours had just extended that list to an uncomfortable length for him. Calling from the hospital to ask the sheriff about William Reiner was just another drop in the question bucket. Maybe that was why Chamblin hadn't fought Foster's desire to leave the hospital earlier than he was supposed to.

"We have questions and we have answers," Chamblin had said, heavy on the vague. "If the good doc is okay with you leaving, then I'd like to use that brain of yours."

Foster and Millie's doctor hadn't been that thrilled at the idea, but Amanda had stuck around to help convince him.

"They're going to the sheriff's department, not a rave," she'd pointed out. "Worst case they pass out among trained professionals, best case they figure out who did this to them and why. But if it sweetens the pot, I will personally go check in on them after my shift."

The doctor had relented—and complimented Amanda's outfit—and added in his off-the-record comment that he believed they'd be fine.

"There's no lingering effects of the drugs, and any physical injuries you obtained were only superficial," he'd said, trying to keep his gaze from settling on his coroner crush. "That said, my unsolicited advice for the near future? If you're looking for leads at a bar, maybe make your own drinks."

That had put fire in Foster's veins. Mostly because he'd been benched while the sheriff's department had gone over every inch of Rosewater and the boat. Including in-depth interviews of staff and patrons. Specifically the bartender.

Foster and Millie had been drugged at almost the same time and, since there were no needle marks anywhere on their bodies, it all boiled down to their drinks.

That was enough to make anyone's skin crawl or, at the very least, uncomfortable, so Foster had felt the need to offer Millie an out.

"I have it on good authority that Deputy Lawrence talks a lot but that he's a good man to have on watch," Foster had told Millie in the hallway after. "He can take you home and keep an eye out while I try to work this at the department."

Millie had been adamant in her short response.

"No way, bud," she'd been quick to say. "We're partners in this now, whether you like it or not."

Foster had had partners before back in Seattle but found that Millie's statement elicited a different kind of reaction from him. But he put that thought on the back burner. It was still sitting there, waiting for more time for him to think on it later, when Deputy Park nodded.

"He's in there with his fifth cup of joe," Park said. "In my nonprofessional opinion? We'd all benefit if a shot or two of whiskey finds its way into his cup."

Foster bet he was right.

Chamblin had come out of semiretirement to become the interim sheriff to help his community, to help his home. To rebuild the department so he could leave it again and be happy with the results. Now he was drenched in a sea of unknowns, and Foster was sure he was getting mighty tired of just treading water.

"Let's drop our stuff off in my office," Foster said, turning toward his closed door.

Chamblin had taken the time to pack a quick bag for Foster when they thought they'd be at the hospital overnight. Larissa, Millie's best friend, had done the same for her. Both had had to use their hidden spare keys, considering Foster and Millie hadn't just lost their memory from the bar, they'd also been stripped of their keys, wallets and cell phones. Millie had mourned the abduction of her purse maybe even more than her own abduction. Then again, Foster understood the grief the first time she'd realized she'd probably never see her things again.

"Fallon's sixth grade school picture was in my wallet," she'd said, voice quiet. "It was my only copy."

Now she was quiet again. Though it was more introspective than upset.

"I can't believe I was sitting in here a week

ago." She set her bag down on the love seat that was crammed into the corner of the office. The piece of furniture was worn and cracked leather, a welcome hand-me-down gift from Chamblin since he knew Foster sometimes spent the night at work when on a case. "It feels like a lot longer."

He chuckled because she was absolutely right.

"You know, growing up I thought Kelby Creek was the most mind-numbingly boring place on the planet. Now here I am with more excitement than a year in Seattle." He checked the top drawer to make sure Fallon's file was still inside. It was. "I guess it goes to show you that even small towns aren't as sleepy as the movies would have you believe. I'd love some boring right now."

A smile passed over Millie's lips but it didn't last. Instead, she followed him down the hall to the sheriff's office, tension lining every move as she went.

They had answers to get. Foster just hoped they weren't all bad.

"Well, if it's not good to see you two up and about." Chamblin greeted them with his, apparently, fifth cup of coffee in hand. He used it to motion to the door. "Let's get rolling and go ahead into the interview room where we can start mapping this all out."

The interview room? Where they interrogated suspects?

Foster raised his eyebrow at that but followed

orders. He got to the door first and let Millie in. Chamblin caught him before he followed.

"Hey, Love, I need you to do me something before we start." His voice dropped so low that Millie couldn't hear.

It tipped Foster off to the fact that he wasn't going to like whatever it was the sheriff was about to ask of him. Millie gave them privacy and took one of the two chairs on either side of the metal table.

Foster didn't like the look of her sitting in the same place criminals were usually handcuffed. He shrugged off the feeling and looked his boss in the eye.

"And what's that?"

"Did Miss Dean ever tell you why she believed the note her brother left was a fake?"

It was such an out of the blue question that Foster took a beat. The sheriff misread his hesitation.

"Listen, Love, I get that you two have been through more thick and thin together than most partners on the force, but I can't just let a civilian into an investigation. Especially not knowing some pretty key facts, like the main reason why she's been looking for a runaway for six months only to have mud slung into the fan the first day we get a new detective in here. For all we know she can be in on this *with* her brother."

There was no hesitation this time.

"No dice there, Sheriff. I may not know what's going on yet, but I do know I trust her."

Chamblin ran his hand along his chin, thinking. The older man wasn't convinced.

"Give me some truth I can work with then. Get her to tell us exactly why she is the only one who thinks Fallon Dean has been in trouble for the last six months, and then I'll tell you why you might not be so quick to trust her."

IT HAD BEEN humid outside, hot too. The Alabama sun was nice to lay out in, but for Millie, that's where her love for it started and stopped.

Inside the interrogation room of the sheriff's department was surprisingly cold. Goose bumps rose up along her arms and pricked up across her legs beneath her jeans. She thought to let her hair down to give the back of her neck some warmth, but Millie wasn't sure the cold in her was all the air conditioner's fault.

Not after the stone-faced Foster took a seat in the metal chair across from her.

And the sheriff didn't come in at all.

Something had changed.

Foster had changed.

He'd gone impassive, unreadable. Just like the first day they'd met with her sitting across from him, frustrated and angry that no one would believe her.

Those feelings tried to come back now.

Millie tamped them down.

After everything she and Foster had been through, she couldn't imagine he didn't believe her.

Unless…

Had something happened while they were in the hospital?

"Miss Dean, I need to ask you something to help clarify a few things for us."

If Millie hadn't seen his lips move, she wouldn't have thought the monotone voice had come from the detective at all.

She glanced behind him at the mirror.

The sheriff must have been behind it. Watching.

Millie felt a wash of embarrassment at not catching on sooner.

They weren't just in the interrogation room to talk. They were in there to question her.

Millie tried to keep the hurt out of her voice as she relented.

"What do you need to know that I haven't already told the department?"

It might have been her imagination, but she could have sworn the detective's jaw hardened. Though the question that followed was a simple one.

"Why do you think the note your brother left you six months ago was fake?"

Millie couldn't help it.

She sighed. Not because she didn't know the answer but because she'd already had this conversation with Detective Gordon. Which meant that the department must not have believed her answer.

Would Foster?

A part of Millie didn't want to know.

If he didn't, then he was just like everyone else.

That was something she couldn't overlook, even after the brushes with danger they'd had together.

"Millie?" he prodded. His golden hair and bright green eyes were harsher beneath the room's hard light. "Can you tell me?"

"Yes. I can and I will, *again*." Her words were harsh too, but Foster was a stone wall. Unmoving and unfazed.

Millie made an effort to soften in comparison, though not by a lot. The story she was about to tell was a long, emotional one.

But it was also the only way to get to her reason.

The reason she knew her brother was in trouble.

"My dad once said that when he met my mom, for the first time, the entire world came into focus," she began. "That up until then the world hadn't been wrong, per se, it had just felt off. My mom was cheesier when she talked about them. *She* said that meeting my dad was like finding the part of her that had been missing, the part that made her whole. Basically they believed they were soul mates. And from what I can remember, I think I could believe that."

Millie paused, just enough to see if Foster planned on interjecting. Wondering why she was talking about her parents being in love, no doubt. Detective Gordon had fussed about it immediately when she'd first told him the story. Foster, however, nodded for her to continue. So, she did.

"That love really carried over to Fallon and me when it came to my dad. He wanted to be, and was, involved in almost every part of our lives. Even when work got in the way, he made sure to always let us know he was there for us. See, he was an adjunct professor of biology at the local community college. He was a big believer in expanding the mind. 'You should never stop trying to learn' was a big motto of his."

Pain, old and profound, started to wake up within her chest. A monster stretching after its hibernation. Millie rolled her shoulders back, trying to physically distance herself from it.

She knew from experience it wouldn't work.

Nothing really would.

"When Fallon was eight he came home so upset," she continued. "It was his first day of elementary school, and he'd found out that they weren't teaching cursive anymore as part of their curriculum. You know, me as a thirteen-year-old didn't get what the big deal was but my dad? He commiserated with Fallon and made him a Dean family promise. He'd teach Fallon cursive himself because you should never stop learning, you know?"

This time Millie couldn't help but shift her entire body. The cold from the room seeped deeper. It burrowed into her bones.

"Dad decided to start teaching Fallon before his Wednesday night class. Since it was a small campus and everyone knew and loved my dad, no one ever really cared that sometimes he would pick us up after school and let us sit in on his class until it was finished. He just really loved spending time with us, even if it was just being in the same room as we did our homework." Millie smiled. It didn't last. "I was out of town on a field trip the afternoon that Jim Mallory decided to take an assault rifle to campus."

Tears pricked at her eyes already. Her throat started to burn. Millie continued anyway while Foster remained impassive.

"He was angry and fast and made it to half of the science department classrooms before he was killed by an off-duty cop. In that time Dad took three bullets shielding Fallon, and he died before the ambulance was even en route."

Millie's vision started to swim. Her chest was tight. Some memories destroyed you, even if they weren't all yours.

"What about Fallon? Was he injured?"

Foster's voice had lost some of the even edge it had when he'd started. It helped bring Millie back to the present.

She cleared her throat and shook her head.

"No, but the damage was more than done," she continued. "It took twenty minutes for authorities to lock down and clear the campus. Fallon spent those twenty minutes holding my dad while he bled out. He wouldn't even leave him when the EMTs came in. One of my dad's colleagues had to physically carry him away so they could do their job." Millie felt relief that that part of the story was done. She knew she could make it through the rest with no problem now. "My mom... Well, she never recovered. I mean we were all devastated, but Mom, she just shattered. I didn't realize it until later, but she was just going through the motions of being a parent after that. She became more like a ghost who haunted the house. An echo of someone who loved us that faded even more every day. If it wasn't for Fallon, I wouldn't have started resenting her for it, but he was just a kid. A scared, traumatized kid who was trying to act like he was okay and his mom didn't even care. I was only thirteen and barely knew how to be a teenager, let alone a parent, and so I did the only thing I could think of to distract him. I decided to teach him cursive."

Foster was at least more engaged than Detective Gordon had been at this point.

"Did he like the idea?" he asked.

Millie actually laughed, her heart becoming lighter at the memory.

"He thought it was the best thing ever," she said. "Every night before bed we'd sit and write in his room until he got it. He likes art, so I think to him it was more like drawing than writing. After he mastered it, he was unstoppable. Every day until I went to college, he'd write me a note in nothing but cursive. That's a lot of letters from me being thirteen to leaving at eighteen, and even after I first got to school he continued to write me these script-filled letters. I told him I didn't expect him to keep it up, but he told me that if I took the time to teach him something, he'd take the time to use it. So, I got a letter every week while I was away. Until I didn't."

She turned her gaze toward the two-way mirror, assuming the sheriff was there.

"You can check the police reports about what happened next. Just like I told Detective Gordon."

Foster's eyebrow rose in question.

"What do you mean? What happened next?"

Millie decided right then and there that this was the last time she ever told this story in its entirety. If they didn't believe her? Well, that was their problem, not hers.

"My mom tried to fill the hole in her heart by

marrying a man named Steve Conway when I was eighteen. Two years later and Fallon stops writing me. One day I get suspicious of how he sounds on the phone, then the next day my mom calls and says he's run away. Since he'd never done that before, I rush home and find him in one of his favorite spots in town. He had bruises all over him. You don't have to be a detective to guess what good ole Steve had been up to."

"He was abusing Fallon."

Millie nodded. "Turns out, not only was it *not* the first time he'd run away, but he'd also gone to the hospital *three* times with mysterious injuries." Millie was angry again. "I filed a report, but by then no one wanted to listen to Fallon. They assumed he was just some teen acting out and hating his stepdad because he wasn't his real dad."

"What about your mom?"

Millie snorted. "She wasn't much better. She went on record saying that she didn't know if she could handle Fallon anymore. Talked about possibly getting DHR involved to get him into foster care so she could get a break." Millie shook her head. "There was no way I was going to let that happen so I left school, got a job in town and made a deal with her that I wouldn't ask for any money from them if she let Fallon live with me until he turned eighteen. She agreed, and the last thing Fallon and I ever did in that place was sit in my car next to the town limits sign and blow out his birthday candle on a cupcake at midnight. Then we ate that cupcake and drove until I found the first Help Wanted sign in a window. We've been in Kelby Creek ever since."

Foster opened his mouth to say something, but Millie wanted to be thorough in her last attempt. She held out her hand to stop him.

"And before you point out that Fallon ran away after we first got here, I'll tell you what I told Detective Gordon. Mom showed up at the house while I was at work one day. She told Fallon she wanted to make sure I hadn't thrown my life away because of him. I got there just as she was leaving and realized Fallon was gone. My then-boss at the grocery store heard me panicking and reported him missing. But this time he had just needed some time to process. To breathe. But the rest, as you know, is history. William Reiner gets hit by a car while Fallon smokes pot in the woods. No one in Kelby Creek has liked him since."

The room filled with silence.

Millie hadn't realized how much adrenaline was pumping through her. She was no longer cold.

Foster was also no longer impassive.

He leaned forward, eyebrow raised again, and put emphasis on the first question he asked.

"And why did you think the note from him was a fake?"

Millie made sure her voice was as clear as crystal as she answered.

"Because it wasn't in cursive."

Chapter Thirteen

"Steve Conway has been booked three times for domestic violence but no charges have ever stuck." Sheriff Chamblin tossed his hat onto a chair next to where Foster was standing. His tone said it all. Disgust at Millie's stepfather. "It seems that Miss Dean was telling the truth about that."

Foster had a hard time not snarling in response.

"I already believed her before she even said a word."

Chamblin sidled up to Foster and gave him a long look. Their reflections were slight in the two-way mirror. He could barely make out the imploring look from his father's old friend in the glass. What he could see clearly was Millie in the next room, tearing the paper off a water bottle and openly trying not to fidget.

Foster didn't like it.

He liked how he'd handled her even less.

"You know, I never thought I'd have to remind you of all people to be objective on a case, but here we are," Chamblin said. "You're working a case. That means asking questions even if it's uncomfortable."

Foster tore his gaze from Millie.

"I'm not uncomfortable with the questions, just how they've been asked and their answers ignored in the past," he countered. "I have no problem with being objective either, but I think that's what's been the problem for the Dean kids since they came to Kelby Creek. Too much objectivity can turn into apathy if you're not careful, and if the law enforcement sworn to help and protect is too apathetic to you, then there's very little chance anything is going to get done the right way."

"Detective Gordon," Chamblin guessed.

"Detective Gordon," Foster confirmed. "Millie said she told him word for word what she told me in there, and he didn't even take the time to put it in his report. Let alone even entertain the thought that she was right about the note. If it had been me? If Millie had come in and told me that same story when Fallon first disappeared? I wouldn't have stopped digging until I hit something."

"So you think Fallon really didn't write it? The note I mean."

Foster crossed his arms over his chest. He was going into a hard stance that his ex-wife used to call Full Detective Mode. Defensive but ready to strike. Walls up, focus engaged.

"I can't say for sure if he did or didn't, but my

guess? If he did, he purposely didn't use cursive as a way to tip Millie off that something was wrong. It sounds like she mostly raised him so he had to have known she would look for him. Either way, I think Fallon is caught up in *something*. I just don't know what yet. But I think it's time I finally talked to Gordon myself."

"You think he knows something."

"He's either incompetent or there's a reason he did such a bad job when he got the case. No matter which one it is, I want to hear it from him. Clearly he knows more than he put in his report."

Sheriff Chamblin let out a sigh so long that it could have rooted into the tiled floor beneath them.

"Gordon is going to have to wait. We have a few more pressing issues." He put his hands on his hips and didn't look pleased at all. Not that either man had looked pleased in days. "We finally identified the two men from the boat."

Foster's ears perked up at that. Since being in the hospital he'd only been updated on their medical statuses. The younger man who had been shot in the leg by Deputy Park had made it out of surgery and was in recovery. The older man had sustained a concussion but would be transferred back into custody once the doctor cleared him.

Past that, Foster felt like he'd been isolated on an island the last several hours while everyone else was on the mainland, so to speak.

"Donni Marsden is the older fellow and Wyatt Cline is the younger one."

Foster tilted his head, trying to jostle a memory loose at either name. Nothing came free.

"I don't think I've heard of or read about them before."

Sheriff Chamblin shook his head.

"I hadn't either, though Park said Wyatt sounded familiar. He went and did a search on social media and found an account for him on Facebook. It hadn't been touched in seven months, but we could see where he loved Auburn football, thought Bill Gates was trying to spy on us all, and frequented a bar in Mobile up until he stopped using the account."

Foster felt his eyebrow raise on reflex.

"Just from what we heard on the boat, I got the distinct impression that he didn't take whatever their job was seriously. And that Donni wasn't a fan of him. Do we know anything else? Mobile is a good drive from here, and Bill Gates does us no good in this situation."

The sheriff snorted and then went serious again.

"Both men have records that were pretty easy to pull up. Though old, Donni Marsden did time for manslaughter back in the nineties down the road in Kipsy and had time added on to his sentence after starting a fight in the prison cafeteria. It was a 'mutual stabbing' according to a guard, and one that left scars on both. After Donni served the extra time and was released, his daughter picked him up at the front gate. That's where Donni Marsden seems to disappear. We couldn't track down anything else aside from an address for his daughter who now lives in Georgia. We reached out to her but so far no luck there either."

Georgia was a state away. Kipsy was a city in the county over. A good drive too, just like Mobile.

And there Foster was thinking that Donni had been a local.

"And let me guess, Wyatt's rap sheet had a whole lot of 'petty' attached to it."

Chamblin gave him a questioning look.

"Petty theft, intoxication, simple assault and disorderly conduct from ages seventeen until last year at twenty-five. How'd you know?"

Foster sighed. "Just a vibe I got from the time on the boat. Plus, if Donni Marsden did time in prison where he got and gave his own hits, I suspect someone who'd only done quick time, if any, wouldn't be someone he respected all that much." That gave Foster an idea. "We might be able to use that. If Donni won't talk, I bet he'd believe Wyatt did. That could get us a reaction from him. He could slip and give us some real info. Have you talked to them yet?"

"Donni clammed up like the devil was trying to tempt him." The sheriff shifted his weight to the other foot. His tone changed to frustrated defeat. "And apparently Wyatt didn't react too well to the anesthesia coming out of surgery. He slipped into a coma."

"What?"

Foster hadn't seen that coming.

"It's rare, I'm told, but it happens. The doc said all we can do is to wait to see when he wakes up. If he wakes up."

"Leaving us with a man who might rather go back to prison than answer any of our questions."

"Unless we can find a way to hit a nerve, I'm thinking that's the gist."

Foster turned back to Millie. She had abandoned her project of stripping the label off her water bottle and was now tracing circles with her finger along the top of the table.

The details.

Foster was good at those. Or, really, he was good at distancing himself from them. So, he made a quick change to the interrogation room and let a new scene play out in his head.

Donni Marsden was sitting where Millie had been, his halo of gray hair centered beneath the harsh light, and Foster across from him.

Donni would growl. He would say that he *wouldn't* say anything. He'd go tight-lipped and he'd cross his arms over his chest, leaning back to show that he rather lounge in the belly of the beast than fret about his luck.

He wasn't nervous or afraid.

He wasn't angry.

He was resigned with a side of sass.

It wouldn't be the first time Foster had to deal with someone like that in a soundproofed room with a metal table in its center.

But that didn't mean it wasn't a challenge. Though at least it was a challenge Foster was used to taking on.

Unlike his and Millie's stint on the boat.

Foster slowly let the image of Donni fade.

Millie was twisting a long curl of her hair between her fingers.

"Is Donni still here?" Foster finally asked.

The sheriff nodded. "In the basement." He clapped Foster on the shoulder. There was a grin in his voice. "Waiting for you."

Foster nodded too. It was more to himself than his company.

"Good because I definitely have questions that need answering. And that woman in there? She deserves them too."

Chamblin turned to face the two-way mirror again. Like Foster slipping into detective mode, he'd gone right into sheriff.

"I'll admit I'm not used to having a case that has so many leads. You're going to have to delegate some of them or you'll just spread yourself too thin."

"And where do you want me to start, boss man?" Foster hadn't meant to, but the words came out with snark attached. Chamblin didn't hold it against him.

"I'd focus on who had the great gall to drug and kidnap a man of the law and his companion from a public place. You pull that thread and follow it, and you might just find out what in the Wild West is going on. And how Fallon might fit, especially after Wyatt name-checked him on the boat."

That was something Foster had spent time in his hospital bed thinking on.

Who was the better opponent that Donni had warned Wyatt about?

And was that the same "him" who had taken Fallon to the boat before Foster and Millie?

"Which means I need to have a lengthy conversation with William Reiner. Again. Preferably one I can remember after the fact."

Chamblin let out one last, long sigh.

"Oh, goody, you have some more news for me?" Foster asked, heavy on the sarcasm. The sheriff didn't take offense, but his mood had definitely soured even more.

"I didn't want to tell you until I knew you were okay and ready to leave the hospital, but we couldn't find him."

"Reiner? What do you mean you couldn't find him? I thought the Good Samaritan who called the department said that Reiner's truck was already gone when she saw us thrown into the one that took us to the boat? Did you send someone to his house?"

Chamblin crossed his arms. "I'm going to glaze by the fact that you're acting like I'm an idiot and didn't immediately look for the man *at his house* and put an all-points bulletin out on him, and instead I'm going to go ahead and dip right into an apology for lying to you earlier." Foster turned his entire body to face the older man. Like the night in the woods, he looked years older than he had the last time Foster had seen him. He nodded toward the two-way mirror.

"You trust her," Chamblin stated. "Why? You barely know her."

Foster didn't know why the answer came so easily.

But it did.

"I just do. Call it a gut feeling. Why?"

There it was. Something that the sheriff had been hiding their entire conversation. Something he'd already had before he'd even directed Foster and Millie into the interrogation room.

Something else had happened while Foster had been in the hospital.

Something that had shifted the sheriff's sense of duty from helping Millie to questioning her.

Now it was like the blindfold had been ripped off. Chamblin went to pick his cowboy hat back up. He wasn't a happy man as he spoke.

"Because, son, if you don't trust her, then this next part might get a little awkward for you." He lowered his voice despite there being no way that Millie could have heard him in the soundproofed room. Not even if he'd yelled. Though his words still rang loud in Foster's ears.

"The truck you and Millie were thrown into was none other than Fallon Dean's."

MILLIE DIDN'T KNOW who Donni Marsden or Wyatt Cline were when Foster reported they'd identified the men who'd drugged and kidnapped them, but she wished she did. If only for the fact that saying she didn't seemed to buy her a one-way ticket to Foster's office.

Since he'd gotten her out of the interrogation room, he'd done a spectacular job of avoiding her. Though if she was honest with herself, he was probably just doing his *actual* job.

And if she was keeping with her self-honesty thing, she was still a bit angry at having to relive the past again in the hopes that someone would do something in the present to help her.

Or she was disappointed.

Millie couldn't decide.

Either way she was quiet when Foster asked her to wait while he did a few things, and she was quiet again when the door to his office opened a half hour later.

"Donni Marsden didn't say a word." Foster ran a hand through his hair and rounded his desk. He pulled open a drawer. Tension lined his shoulders. "I mean, not even *one* syllable." He rummaged through the drawer, obviously looking for something, then abandoned the search altogether.

Finally, he met her eye.

A butterfly dislodged in Millie's stomach at the contact. She saw the man who had risked his life to save her, the one who had bloody knuckles and a cut along his cheek. She also saw the man who had called her Miss Dean before questioning her.

Foster was now a problem for Millie.

He was a distraction, and she didn't need any more of those.

She stood to distance herself from that one butterfly trying its best to sway her.

"And I'm guessing Wyatt hasn't woken up since you left me in here?" Millie overcompensated her attempt to act normal and went right into a bite. Foster didn't address it.

"Yeah. The sheriff said he'd let me know as soon as Wyatt was awake. *If* he wakes up at all."

"Could I talk to him then? Donni."

That earned the quickest *I don't think so* look Millie had ever seen. She felt her expression harden into defiance.

Foster shut the drawer and let out a breath.

"I don't think that's a great idea."

"And why not? Because I'm not a cop? Or is it because I'm a woman?"

Foster shook his head but was interrupted by a knock on the doorframe. Millie turned to see Deputy Park. Since what had happened on the creek, all hostility the man had once had for Millie had disappeared. Though Millie wasn't sure the feeling was mutual yet.

"I'm ready now, if you two are. Deputy Lawrence is already there."

Millie shared a look with Foster.

"Where is there?"

"Rosewater," Foster answered. "He's going to drop us off."

"Why? Did the department find something?"

Excitement became a soothing salve over the emotional turbulence Millie had been experiencing the last several hours. A lead? That was something she'd gladly take.

The tension in Foster's shoulders lessened. He grinned.

"They found something all right."

Chapter Fourteen

"I know I don't have your years of experience in the field, but this isn't normal, is it?"

Millie was standing in the middle of Rosewater Bar, holding her cell phone in one hand and her purse in the other. Foster had his truck keys and phone in his own hands, brow creased in thought. He'd already put his badge back around his neck and his sidearm and holster across his hips. Even his blazer seemed to be in fine shape and was currently draped over a bar stool.

"I just thought whoever took us kept our things or, you know, threw them away," Millie continued. "Not put them in the lost and found box."

Foster ran his thumb along his keys in one hand while scrolling through his phone in the other. As soon as they arrived and Deputy Lawrence had shown them where their things were, Millie had searched her purse. As far as she could tell, everything was still in its place. Including Fallon's sixth grade school picture. The moment she'd seen it Millie had made a silent vow to make a copy of it as soon as possible.

"The whole thing doesn't make much sense," Foster said when he was satisfied with his phone.

He turned to where they had been sitting the night before. The place where both of their memories had run out.

"We decided on a plan with Reiner where you told him that I was your new neighbor and asked you for an introduction since I was the new lead detective at the department," he continued. "Then we went to his table, drinks in hand."

He walked over to where Reiner had been seated. Daylight from the front door streamed in, dust motes visible in the air. Daytime pulled off the mask that Rosewater wore at night. There were no colored lights. No patron chatter mingled with music from the overhead speakers. The bartender was gone, as were any and all staff. Instead of the smell of fries and alcohol, the place stunk of cleaning supplies.

During the day, Rosewater lost all its charm.

It certainly didn't help her overall opinion of the bar that the last time Millie had been inside she'd been drugged.

"I don't remember talking to him," she added, coming up to his elbow, careful to tuck her purse against her side. "I just remember walking. Do you think the drugs had already taken effect that fast? We were only seated for—what?—ten minutes?"

Foster was scanning the area around the table. He shrugged.

"The doc said that those meds can sometimes block out the time before they were even ingested, which makes figuring out a timeline a bit trickier." Foster bent down, inspecting the floor beneath the table. Millie leaned in, curious.

"See anything?"

Foster shook his head. Then his eyes were off to the door behind them, which led to the kitchen.

"After we were reported to have been taken by the Good Samaritan, two deputies were dispatched to question everyone here who had seen us." He was still crouched. It reminded Millie of an umpire about to be asked to make a call. The concentration made her own brow furrow as she tried to picture the bar the night before the best she could. "One couple was sure that we never went to the bathrooms since they were seated near them."

He pointed to the table closest to the bathroom doors but didn't pull his gaze from the kitchen.

"Two different patrons saw William Reiner leave through the front door while we were still inside," he continued. "But of all the people in here, staff included, no one saw *us* leave through the same doors."

Millie stepped back as Foster stood and, without any more of an explanation, seemed to follow his invisible line of thought. She followed him wordlessly to the kitchen door, where he stopped so quickly that Millie ran into him.

A blush burned its way up her neck and singed her cheeks.

"Oops, sorry."

Foster didn't flinch as he looked to the bar.

"Deputy Lawrence said that everyone in here confirmed everyone *stayed* in here except for Reiner."

"Well, drugged or not, I'm pretty sure we didn't just disappear into thin air," Millie pointed out. Though she knew he wasn't implying that they had.

Foster Lovett was in his element.

And he was building up to something.

"You're right. Someone would have seen us if we left through the front door. There were too many people for everyone who had been interviewed to be sure we hadn't gone out that way. So—" he pointed to the kitchen door in front of him but kept his gaze on the bar "—the only other way to leave would have been to go through the kitchen door, and only one person had direct sight line to that at all times."

"June Meeks, the bartender," Millie finished. "But wasn't she questioned extensively while we were missing and in the hospital?"

He nodded. "After they realized we'd been drugged, she was brought in for more questioning. The sheriff himself headed it up. He said he didn't think she had anything to do with it, but I also haven't had a chance to ask her myself. Until then I'm going to trust his call."

Millie thought that was absurd, but she didn't say as much. They were drugged through their drinks, and yet the bartender wasn't suspect because the sheriff said so? And now Foster thought June had seen them leave through the back but lied about it?

Then again, why in the world would June Meeks drug and lie about them?

It made no sense.

Not that much made sense recently.

"So you think June saw us go through the back and then the cook didn't see us?"

Foster shook his head and pushed into the kitchen in question.

"The cook left right after we got here. I remember seeing him when we were at our table. Apparently, his wife had car trouble so he ran out to help and didn't get back until deputies were here."

Millie had never been in the kitchen of Rosewater before, at least not when she remembered it. It wasn't that big of a room but it had three doors. One had a scratched plaque that read Office, the other had an exit sign, and in between them was a freezer door.

"So let's say we *did* come in here, with or without June knowing." Millie motioned to the doors and shrugged. "Why? You said earlier the owner wasn't here at all and now neither was the cook. So why did *we* sneak back here?"

For the first time since Deputy Park had dropped them off, a look that wasn't wholly professional crossed his expression.

He glanced down at her lips.

All at once the kitchen felt like it had shrunk to the size of a shoebox. In it, the space between Millie and the detective became nearly nonexistent. She was still so close to him that she could feel the heat from his arm radiating toward her own.

So close.

And Millie was feeling the urge to get closer.

There was no denying the attraction between them. Not anymore. Not for her.

Millie had been struggling with it since she'd sat down in his office, even after she'd left, angry at him.

She was *attracted* to him.

Plain and simple.

But did he feel the same? Or was he simply following every avenue of thought about the night before?

Millie and Foster in the kitchen with an unspoken attraction instead of a candlestick?

The blush from earlier flared back to life but, regardless, Millie had to set the man straight.

"Listen, if I wanted to *sneak around* with you there would be a lot easier ways and a lot better places to do it." She caught herself with a stammer. "I—I mean not 'do it' but, you know, *seek privacy* with you. I'd pick your truck, if anything. Especially over the Rosewater kitchen, and that's assuming you somehow sweet-talked me into not worrying about the gossip if we got caught."

Foster's lips turned up at the corners. He was trying not to laugh. Which made it only slightly adorable when he finally did. It was a deep, rumbling sound.

He held up his hands in defense and was still chuckling a little as he continued.

"Okay, okay so if we weren't back here for *personal* reasons, then the only other reason I can think of would be because of maybe something Reiner said to us before he left. Or maybe we came in to look for something?"

They lapsed into silence as they split up and searched through the kitchen. Foster went into the office and Millie into the freezer. She didn't know what they might be looking for, but there wasn't anything but food and containers inside. She backtracked and shut the door behind her. She let Foster finish his own search solo and turned her attention to the door leading to the exit.

There was no fire alarm warning attached to it, so she took her chances and pushed it open.

No alarm went off but heat, wrapped tightly in humidity, hit her as hard as the noise would have. Millie growled at it as she walked out onto the concrete pad. A dumpster for the bar sat against the wall, and trees from the overgrown lot that bordered the old motel was opposite, blocking the back lane from being visible to patrons and the parking lot.

Millie went to the edge of the concrete pad and looked down at the ground that continued on from its edge to the back of the middle section of the building. Cigarette butts and footprints were pressed into the damp dirt. They looked relatively new, probably belonging to deputies in the department who were asked to comb the area.

Still, Millie followed, she thought, two different sets of footprints until she was behind the rooms that had been used as storage since the bed-and-breakfast had shut down. Since all the doors to enter the rooms were positioned on the front of the building, she started to look in the windows. They'd been put in during the renovation but looked as worn and stained as the old rooms had been. One of the windows was even missing a screen altogether. Whoever owned the middle section of the building sure hadn't been around to maintain or clean it in a while, Millie decided.

She looked back down the narrow lane toward the bar's back door and then past it to a patch of grass just before it transitioned to the street.

"Why were we out here?" she asked herself out loud.

According to the Good Samaritan, and then according to Foster who heard it from the sheriff, Millie and Foster had been put in a truck in the parking lot in front of the business offices side of the building.

What had happened between the time they had gone into the kitchen to when they'd gotten into the truck?

Why had they been taken in the first place?

Who had Foster fought?

And, with a resounding frustration, Millie came back to the general why of it all.

"Millie?" Foster's voice carried to her, along with its worry.

It was touching.

When she met his gaze, he visibly calmed.

"Did you find anything?" she asked.

He shook his head.

"Nothing remotely out of place or interesting. You?"

Millie motioned to the window closest to them.

"Nothing other than the thought that whoever owns this part of the old motel should probably invest in some Windex."

Foster agreed.

They walked the rest of the length of the building and rounded the corners until they were in the parking lot in front of the business offices.

Nothing popped out and yelled a clue at them.

Which was probably why Foster had gone more tense than when they'd first walked into the bar.

"At least we have our things back," Millie said as they stopped between two yellow painted lines. He was surveying the lot; Millie was surveying him.

Even in profile the man was a sight.

His jaw hardened. Then it was all cool green eyes on her.

"Millie, I need to tell you something about when we—"

"Foster Lovett, I swear to everything holy!"

A woman's voice shrieked through the air behind them. Millie jumped. On instinct she grabbed Foster's arm. The detective, however, looked less startled.

He turned so they were both looking at a woman coming out of one of the offices. He groaned.

"Why is Mrs. Zamboni charging over here at us?" Millie asked. "And why is she so angry?"

Foster made a noise. She couldn't place its emotion.

"Because she's my former sister-in-law and likes being a pain." He lowered his voice and finished in a rush. "And she's like The Hulk. She's always angry."

"I HAVE SPENT almost sixteen years of my life not giving a dog's behind about you, Foster Lovett, and I'd prefer you'd keep it that way."

Helen wasn't wearing her crown of flowers like the day before, but her stomach seemed even more round in her flower-print dress. Her eyes, though, were wide. Foster hadn't seen her so grumpy since she'd turned sixteen and failed her driver's test. Twice.

"Well, how do you do too, there, Helen," he replied.

Millie let go of his arm. Foster wondered if they already knew each other. Being a palm reader in small-town Alabama was pretty close to celebrity status.

But Foster wasn't going to take his chances on not being polite, so he went ahead with introductions before getting to the current root of Helen Mercer's problem with him.

"Millie Dean, meet Helen Mercer. Helen, this is Millie."

Helen stopped with a huff but nodded to Millie. Then she was quickly back on him.

"I do not like feeling anything for you other than some good ole dislike, so you better watch your back around here because I certainly can't keep doing it."

Foster's eyebrow rose.

Helen wasn't her usual mad.

"What are you talking about?"

"I'm talking about being eight months pregnant and trying to chase you two down after you were taken! Philip nearly had a hay day when he saw the damage I made to the car after popping the curb trying to speed after y'all."

Foster put his hand up to slow the woman's rate of words per millisecond.

"Wait." Then it dawned on him. "*You're* the Good Samaritan who saw us get taken?"

Helen gave him a *well, duh* look.

"Not only did I see it and call the department, I chased after that dang truck until it lost me in the back roads! Nearly went into labor over how stressful it was."

Foster could barely believe it.

Helen had saved them, and now? Now she was upset.

She cared.

"Helen, if it wasn't for you, no one would have known we were missing until the next day most likely," he told her. "You saved us."

Foster would have extended a hug had it been anyone else, but he didn't want to invade her personal space, especially her pregnant, personal space. They'd never had that relationship.

But Millie took it into her own hands.

She wrapped her arms around Helen within the span of a blink.

"Thank you," Millie said into Helen's silver hair. "I don't know what would have happened had Deputy Park not gotten to us when he did."

Foster agreed.

Helen's look of grumpiness softened. Discounting her interactions with him, she was a polite, well-liked woman in the town. She patted Millie's back and nodded to her when the embrace was finished.

"Well, I can't very well go on disliking Foster if he's not around to tick me off." Her words had gone softer too. "Plus it looked to me like he was the one doing all the heavy lifting." She glanced down at his hands. They were still bruised and scabbed from his fight.

"You saw me fighting?"

She nodded. "Or trying." Helen pointed to the corner behind them. "The streetlight blew months back and it was dark. Plus you two were on the other side of the truck. Like I told the sheriff, I couldn't make out who you were tussling with, but I could hear, and vaguely see you, hitting him. You seemed slow, though. It didn't look like it took too much to put you in the truck too."

Foster looked down at Millie.

"So then that's definitely our guy," she said, guessing at his thoughts. "The one you bloodied your knuckles on."

The one who might be Fallon.

That's what he'd been about to tell Millie before Helen had interrupted.

The truck they'd been taken in? Fallon's.

Which meant one of two things and neither of them good for Millie.

That's why he kept quiet now.

He wasn't about to give her those two theories in front of Helen.

Despite it being his job, it felt like something he should do in private. Something to talk about with just the two of them.

Helen cleared her throat. Her hand went over her stomach in what must have been a soothing motion. She met Foster's eye with a severe expression and tone.

"You might not be family anymore, but I've grown used to disliking you. If you go up and get killed on me, then I won't have someone to complain about anymore," she said. "Whatever is going on, I need you to figure it out and get it settled. Without getting kidnapped again. Okay? I need this town to go back to normal."

Foster had thought the last week had already been strange enough, but it took another turn as Helen waited for him to confirm he would, essentially, try to stay safe.

"I'll try my best."

Helen nodded. Then she went back to her shop.

They watched as she walked away. Millie was the first to speak. There was no humor in her words.

"I don't think this town has been normal since Annie McHale went missing."

Chapter Fifteen

The water was warm, a gentle hand against the skin of someone who needed to relax. To reflect. To heal.

To try to feel an emotion that wasn't so complicated that she'd pushed away the only man who had been helping her.

Millie slid farther down in the tub, a sigh escaping as she went. Her shower cap crinkled. Water lapped against the back of her neck. The bubbles had already started to dwindle, though their scents of vanilla and lavender had long since coated her skin.

If she closed her eyes and tried to the best of her abilities, she could almost forget about the last week. The last six months too.

Almost.

But that was putting too much pressure on a bubble bath.

Millie opened her eyes and looked at the tile wall opposite her. It wasn't intentional and it certainly wasn't hard to do, but she imagined the house on the other side of that wall.

She sighed again.

Foster had taken them from the parking lot of Rosewater to her front porch, all while staying as quiet as a mouse. Millie had known he was gearing up to say something, something she probably wasn't going to like. It was only after he'd made sure her house was empty and that the deputy at the road was alert, did he circle back to her standing on the front porch and finally said what was on his mind.

"Helen saw and described the vehicle that took us from Rosewater. She even got a partial license plate."

Hope had sprung eternal. A lead!

But then he pulled the cord on that hope with four words.

"It was Fallon's truck."

Millie had felt excitement and anguish all at once.

It hadn't helped that Foster had told her his thoughts on the topic.

"The man who took us could have been Fallon or been working with him, meaning he's not just missing but he's involved in something and choosing not to come forward." Then he'd softened. Sympathy had drenched his expression. Millie's stomach had gone cold. "Or something happened to Fallon and his truck was stolen."

Millie hadn't wanted to sit there and listen to reason or theories. After everything she'd been through in the last week? The last twenty-four hours? Her entire adulthood? Finding out about Fallon's truck—his beloved truck that he'd never give up without a fight or consent—was too much for Millie.

So she'd focused on the part that shouldn't have mattered the most, if at all.

"Why didn't you tell me earlier? Why didn't you tell me when you found out?"

Foster had done his detective thing again. Just like he had in the interrogation room. He'd gone from a man who looked at her with concern and depth to a professional who had deemed her non-essential. Or a threat. His mouth had tightened, his stance had hardened and even his voice had gone almost flat.

"I wanted to know more before I did that."

Millie's heart had been hurting and scared and she knew she'd misplaced her emotions. Still her voice had raised and the corners of her eyes had pricked with tears.

"You wanted to figure out if I had something to do with it too, didn't you? You wanted to see if Millie Dean was just as much trouble as her brother."

Foster had shaken his head. "Millie, that's not it. I just wanted to—"

But Millie had reached the point of no return.

She'd interrupted him by raising her hand to stop whatever it was he'd been about to say to her.

"We're not a team. We're not partners. I'm just your neighbor and a suspect. And I'm tired. I'll make sure my phone is on and all the doors and windows stay shut and locked, but I'm going inside now. I'll talk to you later."

The words had rushed out, but there had been power behind each syllable. Maybe it was that power that kept the man from responding past a nod of acknowledgment and a quiet "okay."

Then he'd gone and now, as night fell, Millie was in the bath, wondering if he was home or not.

Before Foster had come to town, before Fallon had disappeared, Millie had lived a life of routine and normalcy. Now it felt wrong to not be with the detective, sleuthing at his side and waiting for those green eyes to land on her.

The idea of a simple life stayed elusive as Millie refused to give thought about what Fallon's truck did or didn't mean. Fallon was, and always had been, a good kid. A great kid. One with heart and a strength that not even he probably realized he had.

He wouldn't be part of something malicious or bad.

But what did it mean if he wasn't involved in whatever it was going on?

Tears started to prick up again.

Millie ran a hand over her face, water catching in her eyes. She shook her head.

Her brother was still alive and, until she was given proof otherwise, Millie decided she was going to stay optimistic.

She finished her bath with new resolve and slipped into her robe with purpose when the doorbell rang.

Fear and adrenaline went to every area of her body. The power of the bubble bath washed away. She checked her phone to make sure she hadn't missed a call or text.

She hadn't.

Millie tied her robe tight and tiptoed to the living room. She peeked out of the front window, barely moving the curtain. Flashes of Jason Talbot with a gun went through her mind, followed by Foster with a smile.

However, the person standing on the welcome mat was neither.

"Amanda?"

Amanda Alvarez was still wearing her colorful patchwork clothes from earlier at the hospital. She had a paper bag in one hand and held it up and out to Millie in greeting.

"I promised Dr. McCrushing On Me that I'd check on you and the detective, so I'm keeping my promise. *With* the addition of greasy burgers and fries because A, I haven't had a chance to eat yet and B, I'm a big believer in it being good for everyone's mental health to have some guilty pleasure food every now and then." She shook the bag. On cue Millie's stomach growled. Amanda laughed. "Could I come in?"

Millie looked out to the street where her assigned deputy babysitter was still sitting. He made no move to get out of the car. Not that Millie thought the coroner was a threat, but it was still nice to know she wasn't even a suspect.

Plus Millie *was* hungry.

"Yeah, sure. Come on in. Just don't mind the mess."

Amanda followed her in and through to the eat-in kitchen. The other woman laughed as they walked.

"This? If you think this is messy then you'd have a meltdown at my place," she said. "I took this job before I found a place to live, so I'm currently staying in the apartment over the pharmacy on Main. It's the size of a shoebox, a shoebox filled to the brim with boxes of crap I don't need but can't let go of."

She took the seat Millie offered and started to dump the bag out.

"I didn't realize that apartment was even livable," Millie replied. "I work across the street from it at the grocers and haven't seen anyone come or go in years."

Amanda laughed. "The parking is in the back alley and, before me, I don't think anyone had lived there in a while. Let's just say my first week in Kelby Creek was spent elbow deep in cleaning supplies and frustration."

Millie grabbed some plates and napkins and nearly sat down before she heard a crinkle.

"And I'm still wearing my shower cap. Please excuse me while I go change." Millie laughed at herself before going to her room and changing into something less comfortable than her robe but comfortable all the same. She had no plans to leave the house that night. Maybe not even leave the house the next day either. She hadn't decided.

When she padded back into the kitchen, Amanda had set both plates and was chewing on some fries.

"Sorry, I'm starving," she said, waving a fry in the air. "And for all of their grease and calories, fries are my weakness."

"No judgments here," Millie assured her. "My weakness is pie. Like entire pies. I have a frozen one in the freezer as we speak."

"My kind of people."

Millie took the seat opposite and tore into her burger with enthusiasm she hadn't had before. It was like her appetite had come back all at once. She was done with half of the burger before Amanda could ask the question that she'd come over to ask in the first place.

"So other than your love for pie, how *are* you

feeling? Any pain or weirdness? Sudden and new superpowers? The urge to eat human flesh?"

Millie snorted. Even though the coroner was joking around, she could see the concern. Millie appreciated the brevity.

"No superpowers unless you can count my undying optimism," Millie joked back. Then she gave a more serious answer, losing her smile for a more thoughtful demeanor in the process. "My head still feels kind of groggy. Like the aftereffects of taking a Benadryl. But it doesn't hurt like it did earlier. I've also been drinking a lot of water like I was told and taking it easy."

"Nothing else? No paranoia or increased anxiety or depression?"

"Well, in the last week I've had someone break into my home and try to kill me, been drugged and woke up on a boat and lost hours of memory." Millie bit into a fry and smirked to show she wasn't taking what she said as seriously as it was. "Aside from the paranoia, anxiety and depression that goes along with that, no, nothing extra."

Amanda held up her own fry and tipped it to Millie.

"Touché."

They ate a few more bites. Millie glanced over Amanda's shoulder. Once again she imagined the house just beyond hers.

And the man who might or might not be in it.

"So, do you need to go check up on Foster

next or was I the second stop?" Millie tried not to blush but probably didn't succeed.

She felt like a schoolgirl fishing for information on her crush.

Amanda didn't pick up on it, or at least didn't take it that way. She shook her head and spoke around a bite of her burger.

"You're my second stop. I went to the department first to see him since it was next to my precious fries' connection."

So Foster was at the department and not home.

Millie felt a pang of anxiety at that. And something else she didn't have time to think on.

"Is he doing okay too? No more headache or sudden superpowers? No signs of being a zombie?"

There she was, fishing again.

"Nope. He answered about the same as you, actually. The whole anxiety and stress thing was 'just a part of the job.' Very macho with his gun on his hip and the files piled on his desk. So I told him I was on the way to get food and see you. He said he'd call ahead to the guy out front, and I told him he needed to head home soon too."

"Let me guess, he took the suggestion under advisement but didn't say he actually would," Millie guessed.

Amanda laughed. "Actually he said he'd already done his resting at the hospital but would head home when he found a stopping point."

"I haven't known Foster more than a week but that seems to be his way. He's really dedicated to his job. Which is definitely something Kelby Creek needs after The Flood."

Millie dipped into the town's past without meaning to. The Flood had just become so ingrained in residents that it was hard not to hit on the topic on occasion.

Amanda picked up on the mood change. She didn't brush it off or make jokes anymore.

"You know, I thought the first person I heard say 'The Flood' was being dramatic, but that's what everyone here in town calls it, isn't it? Everything that went down?"

Millie finished her burger with a last bite. She nodded. Amanda waited until she was done chewing to press on.

"You were here for it? The Flood?"

"Yeah." Millie was also there before it had happened long enough to feel the burn, the hurt, the betrayal.

The anger.

"I don't know who started the name, but it's been the easiest way to refer to what happened," she added. "Plus the flood *is* what really changed everything."

Amanda's brow rose high.

"It's not just a metaphorical name?"

Millie shook her head and paused in the process of getting more fries. She knew the look that crossed Amanda's face just as she'd seen the same one in her reflection over the last six months.

"Do you not know what happened?" she asked. "You replaced someone who was fired because of it."

"I only know the highlights that the news gave out. And, well, that my predecessor was fired for fudging reports, but I never got the *details* details. Not the up close and personal ones."

Amanda's expression was searching. Since Millie had already decided she liked the woman, she relented and told the story of The Flood.

Well, after she got out the frozen pie to let it thaw.

Then she told the coroner to buckle up because she was jumping right on in.

"There are two really wealthy families in Dawn County. The McHales were one of them and had lived in Kelby Creek for generations. They had family money and then they made more by having a hand in half of the town's businesses. But, for all the stereotypes of the rich family being small-town royalty, the McHale family was actually very beloved. If you didn't know they had a veritable mansion in the woods, you might not know they were filthy rich at all. That went doubly for their only daughter, Annie McHale."

Millie paused to do some math, trying to remember the exact timeline.

"Everyone refers to the beginning of the end for

a normal Kelby Creek when Annie went missing, but the truth was she was actually kidnapped," she continued. "It's just that no one knew for sure until a few days had passed and missing, I suppose, sounds less menacing compared to what actually happened. Annie went missing on a Sunday and by Wednesday a ransom call was made to her parents. The kidnappers wanted five hundred thousand dollars within twenty-four hours or they'd kill her."

Amanda made a noise. "That's some kind of action stuff you see on a TV show."

Millie had to agree with that.

"It only gets more intense from there. See, the McHales were really close with the sheriff. He was actually the kids' godfather. So when the call came in and a drop for the money was set up, he convinced the McHales to let him be the one who handled it. He took some undercover deputies with him and led them and Mr. McHale right into a trap." Millie didn't say it, but she remembered hearing the gunfire from the store that day. Like fireworks popping in rapid succession until there was nothing but an eerie silence. "In total five people were killed, some deputies and some civilians while a few more were wounded. Mr. McHale even took a bullet to the leg and nearly bled out."

"What about the kidnappers?"

"They managed to stay hidden, is what everyone said at the time. But after that the kidnappers became openly angry and pulled the stunt that put the town on national news and finally brought in the FBI."

"I know this part," Amanda said excitedly. "The town website got hacked."

Millie nodded. "A video of Annie McHale was posted on the website and stayed up for half an hour until someone could get it down. It went viral across the internet."

"I saw it. She was just sitting there all bloody and beaten tied to a chair while some guy spoke next to the camera. He asked for more money, didn't he?"

"A million dollars this time," Millie answered. "And three days to do it in."

"Let me guess. After her parents saw the video, they were definitely in."

"Oh yeah. But they didn't get the chance to actually do it." Millie couldn't help but lean in a little, as if she was conspiring with Amanda. This part of the story always felt a little unreal. "Two FBI agents came in as part of a small task force to help and, the day after the video was posted, one of the agents, Jaqueline Ortega, left a message on her partner's phone that she was following up on a hunch. But then she went missing too."

"What? I never heard about that part."

Millie shrugged. "Jaqueline Ortega, as far as I could see, never made the news. *But* her partner did," she continued. "He was out looking for her the next day, driving through some backroads, when a nasty storm hit. It created a flash flood and by the time he had decided to go back to his hotel room, he came up on a car that had wrecked out into the ditch. Being the good guy he was, he stopped to help them. Turns out, it was the mayor. Good friends with the sheriff and the McHales. He was unconscious but alive and while the FBI agent saw to him, he spotted something shiny in the floorboard. A necklace specifically designed for Annie McHale."

Amanda sucked in a breath. "Man, this story needed popcorn, not fries! So that's how everyone was caught? The mayor wrecked because of a flash flood?"

Millie nodded. "Apparently the wreck dislodged the necklace and it was all the FBI guy needed," Millie confirmed. "He launched his own investigation, and then all the pieces started to come into place. The sheriff and the mayor had been the masterminds behind the kidnapping and ransom. They'd also been behind the ambush and the video."

"And they weren't alone."

"Nope. Not by a long shot." This part of the story was widely known, but Millie recapped it for completion sake. "A new FBI team came and started a town-wide investigation of local law and government to see how deep the corruption went. Annie McHale was just the tip of the iceberg. Several people were fired, some were incarcerated and a few even ran. It took nearly a year to sort everything out and, then, the FBI just left. The town hasn't trusted local law or government since."

"That's why Foster and I are here," Amanda added.

"Yep. The town needs redeeming, most especially the sheriff's department."

Amanda let out a long, deep breath. She finally stuck her fork in the piece of pie Millie had offered.

"That's a tall order," she said. "Trying to get an entire town to trust you."

At this, Millie felt a coldness in her.

"It doesn't help that Annie McHale and Jaqueline Ortega were never found."

Amanda didn't disagree.

After that the two women ate their pie in silence.

Chapter Sixteen

Foster dropped his keys on the kitchen counter and tried his best not to swear.

It wasn't like anyone was in his house to hear him if he did. The AC was the only thing that stirred when he came through the front door, and a beer from the fridge was the only thing calling his name.

He put away his badge and gun and got that beer, popping the cap with a little too much force and a whole lot of frustration.

Kelby Creek had gone from his hometown to home of his most complicated case. He couldn't figure it out and he couldn't escape it. Not that he wanted that. Foster went to the dining room window and peered out into the night.

From the driveway he'd been able to see Millie's living room light was on, but he couldn't see any movement. He had no idea what she was doing or *how* she was doing.

And it bothered him.

And it bothered him that it bothered him.

We're not a team. We're not partners.

Millie had been right. She was his neighbor. She was also a victim or a suspect, depending on who you talked to. But in his eyes? Millie hadn't asked for any of this to happen to her. She hadn't planned any of what they'd been through. Foster felt that truth in his bones. Now he was looking for answers, justice, and a way to give the woman who deserved some good, some kind of peace.

Foster should have told her that on the porch. Should have hammered home that she wasn't a suspect to him, but the way Millie had looked at him? It was like he'd watched a piece of her break right there on the same spot he'd been shot the week before. Foster hadn't known how to react because he hadn't known the cause. So, what did you do when you didn't know what to do?

He hadn't done anything at all.

Which meant now he shouldn't have wanted to update her on what he'd found. He shouldn't have wanted to talk through everything that had happened to her. He *definitely* shouldn't have wanted to go next door and forget about the case for a while.

But he did.

"Women are trouble, Foster," he reminded himself and the still-somewhat-stale air of his new home around him. "That one with a capital *T.* Pull it together. Do your job."

The pep talk carried him to the hallway bathroom. He turned the shower on and put his beer on the counter. The reflection in the mirror showed him a man who was tired but wasn't about to sleep. Not until he had answers.

Just one.

That was why he was in Kelby Creek. To help the department, to help the town. Not to stumble through his first investigation since he got back.

For Pete's sake, you got shot and drugged within the first week!

Foster shook his head at himself. This time he did curse.

It was back to the drawing board when he got out of the shower, he decided. He needed to rethink everything from tip to tail.

He could do this.

He *had* to do this.

Foster nodded his affirmation to himself and started to pull up the hem of his shirt to undress. Instead, he watched his reflection flinch. Without any pain meds in his system, his bruised ribs had become angrier. Painful. Especially since Donni Marsden had used him as a punching bag on the boat. Donni might have been older, but he'd had force behind each blow. It also didn't help Foster's case that the sheriff had grabbed a casual T-shirt and not a button-up to put in his hospital bag.

"Can't solve this case, can't take off your shirt," he grumbled.

He switched sides, hoping that would help the pain.

It didn't.

He was considering getting the scissors when the doorbell rang.

"Coming!"

Foster glanced at his phone on the kitchen counter on the way to the door—no new messages—and went right for the peephole. He imagined the sheriff being on the other side, ready to share a beer and frustration. Maybe talk over the case some more and discuss how to deal with Donni Marsden and Fallon's still-missing truck.

But the sheriff and his cowboy hat weren't on the other side of the door.

All at once, Foster went on alert and quickly pulled open the door.

"Millie? Are you okay?"

Millie didn't appear to be in any physical pain or trouble—in fact, she looked like she'd been getting ready for bed in a worn cotton tee and a pair of sweatpants—but there was nothing but distress written across her face.

Foster looked over her shoulder. Deputy Calloway's cruiser was still at the curb. No one else seemed to be in the street or around the yards.

"What's wrong?" he prodded when she still hadn't answered. Foster pictured his gun locked in the nightstand next to his bed. Too far away if he needed to act fast. He'd just have to use his fists.

Millie's wide eyes managed to widen a bit more. "Oh, no. I'm okay," she hurried to say. "I just wanted to talk. Sorry. Can I come inside?"

Foster didn't lower his guard just yet. He stepped aside, not moving until she was past him.

"Sure, yeah, come in."

The smell of lavender and something else mixed in surrounded him. Foster tamped down the urge to enjoy the scent. It was one he was becoming used to. He instead focused solely on the woman and whatever it was that had her upset.

Which wasn't hard considering she stopped in the middle of the open room and whirled around to face him with such acute worry, Foster went right back to high alert.

"Is that the shower going?" she asked, voice pitched higher than normal. Her gaze trailed down to the beer in his hand. He hadn't realized he'd swiped it from the counter next to the sink. "Oh, are you not alone? Is someone else here? Am I interrupting?"

The way she said that made it sound like Foster had a lady friend lying in wait. He laughed the idea off.

"No, no one's here. The only thing you interrupted was me about to drink in the shower and, honestly, that's probably a good thing."

Millie looked a little less distressed, but not fully relieved. Foster sidestepped offering her a beer to get to the reason behind the late visit.

"Millie, what's wrong?"

The AC revved to life and the ice maker in the refrigerator dropped some ice cubes. Foster even heard some frog chirping outside the window. All before Millie worked up enough courage to saying what she'd come to say. She opened her mouth then closed it. She did it again.

There were tears in her voice.

"Annie McHale was gone for two hours before Kelby Creek turned upside down. Less than a week later the entire country wanted to find her, to know what happened." Those tears warbled her normally calm voice. "Fallon was gone for three days, and I had to *beg* for someone to listen to me. Fallon has been gone for six months and no one seems to care about what happened but me. That is, no one until you. But, honestly, if I hadn't gone to the woods that night? If Jason Talbot hadn't come for me? I'm not even sure you would have given Fallon, or me, another thought."

Foster tried to interrupt but she kept on. She wrung her hands.

"I mean no disrespect or lack of appreciation for what you've done so far. It's just that when you told me about Fallon's truck, I couldn't figure out what to feel." She took a step closer to him. "Ever since my dad was killed, life hasn't stuck to any plan I've ever made. School, a future career path, serious relationships, my mom? I learned to roll with the punches as a way to survive because I know things could always be worse. Then, eventually, the only constant in my life became Fallon. He's been my person since he was that ten-year-old boy sitting on his bed practicing cursive."

She took a breath. When she spoke again, her voice was not as tremulous.

"I have tried very hard to make sure he has the stability that we never had growing up. I've tried to make Kelby Creek a real home, to build a foundation that he can always come back to when he's ready. But then? Then he was just gone. And nothing I had done, nothing I *have* done, seemed to matter anymore." She paused. Foster was surprised to see one of her hands fist at her side. "I've spent the last six months trying to find Fallon because I love him, because I want him to be safe, but—in a small way—I don't know who I am without him. Every choice I've made, every decision I've come to in the last several years has been as a sister, as a surrogate mom, as a moral compass. It's been for Fallon, for our family."

Millie stood straighter. Like she'd been zapped by a sudden surge of electricity. Her hands relaxed though her gaze sharpened.

She was no longer on shaky ground.

She was determined.

"But it wasn't until today when I stood in front of you and felt like a suspect that I realized how much your opinion matters to me. How, even though you wouldn't be the first and probably won't be the last person to not believe me, to not trust me, you're the first person I've actually wanted to prove wrong. Not out of spite but because I like being around you. Not as a sister. Not as a guardian or teacher. Me as Millie. I know that probably seems a bit weird considering I barely know you, but it's the truth."

She put her hands on her hips, determination mounting.

"So, all of this was to say, I'm sorry I snapped at you earlier when you were just doing your job. I just— Well, for a lot of reasons, I didn't want this to end. I'm sorry."

Foster watched as Millie let out an exhale that relaxed her rigid stance. Instead of defeat or embarrassment, she seemed relieved.

Then she was waiting.

Waiting for him to respond.

Little did she know that Foster had already come to a conclusion about Millie before she ever set foot inside his house.

Foster smiled. He hoped she saw how genuine it really was.

"Millie Dean, I have never thought you were anything other than extraordinary," he said, honest. "You're too good for this town, for me, and certainly for anyone who has the gall to think you're less than. I wouldn't keep my distance from you unless you told me to do so. Case or no case."

There it was. The truth. It wasn't as eloquent as Millie's or as deep, but it was how Foster felt.

He might have only known Millie a week, but in that time she'd spent every moment they had together proving that she was a woman to be reckoned with. A warrior with a heart of gold. Someone you were lucky to have by your side in thick or thin or otherwise.

Foster figured he should say that, but Millie made a fool of his detective skills. In a move he truly didn't see coming, Millie closed the space between them and covered his lips with hers. Bruised ribs be damned, Foster didn't move an inch as she pressed against him.

Then it was like she was electrocuted again. She ended the kiss and backed up in a panic.

"I—I'm sorry. I just wanted to do that and realized that maybe you were just being nice and professional and then here I was lunging at you after invading your house!"

In that moment Foster could have done a lot of things.

He could have been professional and told her not to worry but yes, they should focus only on the case for now.

He could have been friendly and assured her

that it was just a kiss in a high-pressure situation, and not to read anything into it.

He could have lied and told her that she'd misread his compliments as something more than they were.

He could have told the truth, spelled out the fact that, as much as he admired Millie, he was attracted to her too. That he was a bit upset he hadn't been the one to kiss her first.

Yet Foster didn't want his words to do the talking.

So he asked her a question instead.

He grinned. When his words came out, they were low and filled with unintended grit.

"Millie Dean, why don't you help me take my shirt off and I can show you just how I feel?"

Millie, God bless her, didn't take long to pick up what he was trying to put down.

Instead of being shy about it, though, she surprised him with a smirk that nearly made him lose his cool right then and there.

"Well, considering I helped you put it on this morning in the first place, I guess it would only be fair to help take it off."

And boy, did she do just that.

Chapter Seventeen

The shower became background noise.

Millie barely registered it. She'd only noted it at all because she expected them to trail that way. Not that she had thought helping the detective take his shirt off because of an injury would lead them directly into the steam together.

Though she'd be lying if her mind wasn't already playing through the logistics of it. Chief among them the fact that there was a good height difference and that her curls would get wet.

But the synapses firing in her head, trying their best to piece together coherent thought, decided whatever happened next with Foster, she was good with. She didn't mind if it was on the floor, in the bedroom, or on the roof.

She wanted him.

More than she'd wanted anyone else in the same sense.

Thankfully, the feeling seemed to be mutual.

The second Millie had his shirt off, Foster was cradling her head in his hands, pulling her close and keeping her against his lips. Millie ate it up. She put her arms around him, steadying them, while her hunger burned through her and out to him.

What started as a warm, introductory kiss deepened. He parted her lips and her tongue searched him out. A moan escaped her lips as he moved his hands down her body, looping one around her back while the other anchored at her hip.

For several blissful moments they were caught in a whirlwind of movement and gasping for air.

Then Foster made a noise.

Millie stopped in an instant.

With hooded eyes and swollen lips she was all concern.

"Are you okay? What's wrong?"

Foster still had his arm around her but dropped the one from her hip. He used it to give her a dismissive wave.

"I'm good. I'm fine."

Millie shook her head. "No one who is good or fine says they're both good and fine. Tell me."

Foster sighed. Then he made a face.

"If I tell you then we might stop, and I don't want to do that," he said.

Millie gently wiggled backward out of his grip. She felt guilty in an instant as she realized what was happening.

"Foster! Am I hurting you?"

She had to give it to the man, he was able to look sheepish and devilishly sexy all at once. Beneath Foster's shirt was a lean but muscled body. Something she'd already seen in the hospital but, after feeling its power against her, a work of art she appreciated much more now. Yet among those muscles and smooth skin was an awful smattering of color.

Bruising from Jason Talbot's bullet.

And from Donni Marsden's fists.

That wasn't even accounting for what she couldn't see.

Not to mention, she'd just had to help take his shirt off.

"I'm fine," he repeated. "The pain caught me a little off guard, is all."

Millie shook her head then traced his side again with her eyes.

That's when she saw the scar farther down, right above the brim of his jeans. It looked like it had once been deep. It was also shiny. Millie had only seen a scar like that once before on her former manager's arm at the store. It had been made by a deep cut. She ran her index finger along the line, like a moth to a flame.

It was a clear reminder that she didn't know much about the man. But that she also wanted to learn.

"That happened a long time ago." His voice had gone low again. Millie absently wondered if it was because of her touch. Even her own tone had changed.

"From Seattle?" She imagined the man in a wild fight with fancy men in suits with misting rain and clouds as a backdrop. Foster, the brooding detective ready to dispense justice. It was an image right out of a television show.

It also was being muscled out by another thought. Foster, however, spoke first before it could fully form.

"I actually got it here in Kelby Creek." He smirked. "From our very own Mrs. Zamboni. Before she was all-knowing, she was a teen with really bad aim and—"

Foster stopped talking. His body went rigid and his green, green eyes widened.

Millie wasn't much better.

The thought that was teasing her fully formed.

It was only the luck of timing that she spoke first.

"When Jason was in my house, he told me that he'd been watching me for weeks and he specifically said in the woods that he'd seen me at the store." She felt a smile pull up her lips, excitement breaking through. "Does that mean we could look at the security camera footage to see him and use that to help us figure something out?"

Foster laughed.

Really laughed.

Millie would have been offended had he not hurried with an explanation.

"That could definitely help us get a lead," he said. "Just like the realization I just had might help us."

"You thought of something too?"

Foster placed his hand over hers, still touching his scar.

"You've got the magic touch, apparently."

Millie laughed. "First time I've heard that but I'll take it. What did *you* realize?"

To say the man was excited was an understatement. He looked like a boy in a candy shop with his mom's credit card.

"Helen, the all-knowing Mrs. Zamboni," he said simply.

That surprised her.

"Wait, you want to ask her for psychic advice?"

This time Foster laughed.

"No, but *William Reiner* went to her with questions about his brother after he left town."

Millie raised her eyebrow. "You think that Reiner is looking for his brother?"

"He was then," he said. "Maybe if we know what questions he asked, we can figure out what he did next when he didn't get any answers from her. Maybe we can find out what he's been up to since, and where he might be now."

Millie nodded.

"Or this could be just what we needed to finally get us on the same page as everyone else," Millie said.

They lapsed into a thoughtful silence. To any outsiders they might have looked odd. Standing in the middle of the living room, Foster shirtless and Millie pressing against his scar, both with red lips.

But they were both invested in everything that had happened so far. More so than anyone else.

They'd been attacked, drugged, questioned and confused.

Finding two new avenues to look down? Well, that was two kids in a candy shop combined with a toy store. The possibility that they might find exactly what they needed was thrilling.

Millie wanted to get started now, and she couldn't imagine that Foster felt any differently. That said, she also was well aware that the time was nearing eleven at night.

Foster had already found his way to the thought, it seemed. He answered her next question aloud.

"I'll make some calls first thing in the morning," he said. "There's nothing we can do with either point tonight."

Millie nodded. Then she asked a follow-up question.

This time she knew the answer. Still, it gave her a thrill to ask it.

"So, what do we do now?"

Foster's mouth quirked up at the corners. When he took her hand and started to walk to the hallway, it felt like a thousand butterflies were fluttering around Millie's stomach.

"I can think of a few things."

Pain? What pain?

Foster didn't seem to feel anything other than Millie once they made it to his bed.

She felt curiosity and appreciation from him as he watched her throw off her shirt to match him. She felt excitement and anticipation as she took it a step further and stripped down to her black silk undies that she'd put on by sheer luck. Then it was wide-eyed, grinning fun as he did a two-step and showed her he was a boxer briefs kind of man.

Nothing but strength followed.

Foster picked up Millie's mostly naked body and brought her with him into a swath of fabric. His hands moved just as fast as his mouth covered hers.

He tasted like beer but also something more. Something she liked.

And Millie wanted more.

His hand found her breast, his fingers her nipple. He teased her, kissed her, and the entire bedroom heard her feelings on it all as another moan escaped. It seemed to hit the right note in the man.

Things escalated and it wasn't one-sided at all.

As Foster's hands went exploring again, Millie decided she was ready for the main adventure. She wrapped her legs around him and spun. It broke their kiss but earned a surprised laugh from the detective.

Her curls shifted as she looked down on the man she was now straddling.

Green eyes searched her face. Then he cupped her cheek, running his thumb along her jaw.

"See?" he said. "Extraordinary."

And that was the magic word.

Millie was smiling as she pressed her lips back to his.

SHE WENT INTO the house and didn't come out until it was morning.

He knew because he was at her kitchen table for hours. Waiting.

You could go next door, he thought. *If you take her, then the detective will follow anyway. Eventually.*

But, ultimately, he decided against it.

Getting into Millie's house without being seen had been easy. Getting into the detective's house would be trickier.

He couldn't change it.

Not now.

So, he waited instead.

When the birds started chirping and the sun started to paint the sky, he admitted defeat. It was only when he was back in the car and driving past the house and the deputy's cruiser that he saw a glimpse of the two, now going into Millie's.

It was a good thing he hadn't stayed, he realized.

There was no way the detective would let Millie go without a fight.

He'd already proven that by killing Jason Talbot.

Now the plan would have to change.

And his boss wasn't going to like that.

Not at all.

"So, Deputy Calloway probably knows what we did last night, doesn't he?"

Millie started the coffee maker, sliding the thermos Foster had brought with him to her house into the holder. The blissful smell of coffee was enough to give her a zip of energy. Though after spending a good portion of the night *not* sleeping, she'd need a bit more than a zip to make it through the day.

Foster, now dressed to impress in a flannel button-up that was open to show his dark undershirt, a pair of Levi's that hugged, and black-and-white Converse running shoes that gave off punk band vibes, chuckled at her comment. Mostly because he probably knew it was true.

She'd walked to his house in the middle of the night and hadn't come home until the morning. Foster was wearing new clothes, and she was wearing his shirt instead of the one she'd arrived in.

Law enforcement or not, that didn't take much detecting skills to figure out what might have happened behind closed doors.

"According to the sheriff, Calloway is a good guy. Professional," Foster said. "I trust that he won't gossip on what he thinks might or might not have happened."

Millie shook her head. Her curls were a different level of wild. Their time spent in bed, then the shower, then back in bed hadn't helped. Foster's hair, however, was model-worthy. Golden, wavy and nothing but complimentary to the rugged handsomeness of a man who was ready to save the day.

Even if it was barely seven in the morning.

"While this brews, I'm going to go get decent," Millie announced.

It earned a sly smile from the man.

"I think you're already more than decent right now."

Millie rolled her eyes.

The level of comfort with the detective had more than risen in the last few hours. Not only physically. Admitting that she hadn't been living for herself had opened up the floodgates for a lot of pent-up emotion for her. Emotion she hadn't realized had tangled up with Foster as much as it had.

He might not have had any big breakthroughs with her in turn, but that didn't matter.

Not last night.

Not right now.

If Foster needed time to lower some of the walls that seemed to always be present, then that was okay.

Millie might want to live for herself, but that didn't mean she was over finding Fallon.

If anything, she was more determined than ever.

Somewhere between talking with Foster and sleep the night before, Millie had decided on one thing and one thing only.

Fallon wasn't involved in what was happening.

He was a good kid. A good man.

Which put even more fire in her to finally get the story. Finally find her brother.

And Millie believed that Foster was the key to it all.

Even as she retreated from the kitchen to go to her bedroom, she could see the detective going from charming to focused.

Their night together had been great but now it was time to get back to work.

What happens when it's all done? The thought was surprising and loud as it rang through Millie's head without warning. *When the danger and mystery are gone, will Foster go with them?*

Chapter Eighteen

The day started out calm enough.

Deputy Park and Millie went to the grocery store to ask for the security camera footage from two weeks before she met Jason Talbot in the woods, then returned to the department to go through it. Foster meanwhile went to talk to his ex-sister-in-law about her time with William Reiner. For all the resentment Helen had harbored through the years at Foster, she was more than willing to help.

"If knowing what Reiner asked will help you stop whoever drugged and kidnapped you and Millie, I'll tell you everything," she'd said. Then, like it was a tic, she'd run her hand over her pregnant belly. "I love this town and I just want it to be safe for my kids."

Helen had taken him into her office, and among colorful tapestries and crystals had broken down the four questions William Reiner had asked.

It was only after he was leaning against the wall of the break room at the department that he was able to repeat them to Deputy Park and Millie.

"Where did Cole Reiner go the day before he left town? Where was Cole now? Did Cole find what he was looking for? Was Cole in danger?"

Foster finished off his coffee and waited for the two to mull over the questions. A laptop was up between the pair, and both had notepads in front of them. Millie might not have been in law enforcement, but she sure was getting to work like the rest of them. A lot more thrilling than her shift at the grocery store. One that Larissa had been kind enough to cover for her.

"It almost sounds like Reiner is treating his brother like a suspect," she said, head tilted to the side and brows drawn together. "But he wasn't found guilty of anything to do with The Flood, right?"

"There was never any evidence found," Foster stated. "Just suspicion with the timing and how fast he left."

Deputy Park shook his head. "No way was Cole mixed up with any of that," he said. "I came into the department with Cole, and he was a straight arrow. He had to be to live up to William's hype, especially once he had to retire." Millie squirmed a little in her seat, but the deputy went on without noticing. "Even you would have liked him, Love. He was trying to make detective before he left."

Foster pushed off the wall. "Cole Reiner wanted to be a detective?"

"Yeah," Park answered with enthusiasm. "I caught him looking into cold case files one day after his shift ended, and he said he was trying to show initiative. I asked what for, and he told me he wanted to make detective."

"That was absolutely not something I knew."

Foster had up until then been on the same wavelength as Millie when it came to Reiner. He had suspected his brother of being involved in The Flood. But now? Now he was switching gears.

"What if we've been looking at this all wrong?" he asked. "What if *Cole* wasn't a suspect during The Flood but instead he was playing detective?"

Millie was quick. "You think he might have been looking into a cold case?"

Foster shrugged. "He could have actually found something in an old file and followed it. Followed it until he had to leave town. Or was forced. It might account for why he left so suddenly."

"Like Fallon."

Millie's voice was small. Deputy Park looked between them. Foster pressed on through the line of thought.

"Let's speculate wildly for a second here." He took a seat in the chair across from them, hands already up and moving with enthusiasm as he worked through the new theory aloud. "William Reiner asked Helen where Cole went the day before he left town. He must have known, or at least suspected, that Cole was working *something*. Which is why he asks her the follow-up questions of where Cole was then, did he find what he was looking for, and was he in danger. Since I got here, nothing about what's happened has really added up. It feels like we just keep getting curveballs thrown at us during this investigation into what happened to Fallon." Foster couldn't help but smile, knowing it was a stretch but one he felt good making as he said it. "What if *we're* the ones who are throwing a curveball into someone *else's* investigation?"

Millie's head was still slightly tilted in curiosity. He could tell she was working through his pitch. Deputy Park was more vocal with his thought process.

"You think someone else is investigating Fallon's disappearance?"

Foster shook his head. "It feels more like we stumbled onto something else *while* looking into Fallon. That's why nothing is fitting. It's not that we don't have all of the pieces, it's that we're not even on the same game board."

At that Millie started.

"'This ain't a game. If it was, we'd be losing to a much better player.' That's what Donni said on the boat," she recalled. "Maybe you're right. Maybe we're the ones who stepped in late."

Deputy Park shook his head this time. He crossed his arms over his chest and leaned back.

"I'd say you two were on the front lines. Someone did drug and kidnap you. Why else would they do that?"

Millie's eyes widened in excitement as an idea took shape.

"To buy them time," she stated. "We weren't hurt, when we woke up we were unsupervised, and since all of our belongings were fine back at Rosewater, all we lost was the time it took for you to find us."

This time the excitement moved to Foster.

He leaned in. "It was like we were put in time-out. We were sidelined."

Millie mimicked his movement. Her leaning in would have frayed his concentration now that Foster knew what she felt like, tasted like, but them being onto something together was a different kind of excitement that was hard to resist.

"Which means that someone didn't want to hurt us, they just want us out of the way."

"But who *is* that someone?" Deputy Park joined them by rocking forward in his chair and leaning closer. "William Reiner? Cole Reiner? Fallon? And how does Jason Talbot fit into any of that?"

At that, Foster lost some of his enthusiasm.

But not all of it.

"We need to keep digging," he decided. "Did you find anything on the security footage so far?"

Deputy Park sighed but Millie answered.

"No. Jason said he saw me the day I was wearing an orange hair clip but, if he came into the store, he did it through the back. We couldn't find him on the street either. We still have two days before that to go through, though."

Foster stood up, a to-do list updating in his head.

"Let me know if you find anything. If you don't, come get me when you're done."

Millie uncapped her pen. Foster focused on the deputy.

"Do you happen to know which cold case file Cole Reiner was looking at when you walked in on him?"

The department had an outstanding amount of cold cases, and that was before all the town-wide corruption had been uncovered. Since then several closed cases had been reopened and then re-routed to cold case status. Dealing with the sheer volume of them was one of Foster's main goals within his new job.

"I never saw the name of the specific one, but I did see the box. Fall 2012." Park snorted. "And the only reason I remember *that* is because we talked about how dumb it was for someone to label the boxes by seasons and not dates."

Foster might have found the humor in that had he not already guessed finding a file that might or might not have been of interest to Cole was going to be a long shot.

Still, it was an actionable lead since everything else had hit dead ends.

Donni still refused to talk, Wyatt was still in a coma, Jason was dead, the boat had been stripped and searched with nothing of value found, and Fallon, William Reiner, and both of their trucks were still missing.

Cole Reiner felt no more or less attainable as a lead as the rest to Foster.

"I'm going to go see if any cold cases pop out at me. Best case, we get lucky and can tell what he was looking at. Worst case, if he found anything in those files, he took it with him."

"And what happens if it's worst case?" Millie asked. "What happens next?"

Foster didn't realize he already knew before his gut said the words for him.

"I'm going to figure out what the hell happened with Cole Reiner."

FOSTER HADN'T FOUND any cold cases that he thought Cole would have found interesting and, according to the list assigned with the box, there were no files missing. From there he'd gone to trying to find out what Cole had been up to since leaving town.

Based on how much he swore when he didn't think Millie could hear him, that hadn't gone well. Foster went from online searches and phone calls to reaching out to current and former sheriff's department employees who might have seen or heard something like Deputy Park had.

Millie hadn't had much better news.

The security footage of the grocery store had shown several locals and residents going into the store but none had been Jason Talbot. The only familiar faces she and Deputy Park had seen belonged to June Meeks, the Rosewater's bartender, Detective Gordon, the sheriff and Larissa. Not as significant as finding Talbot would have been. It was a small town, after all. Familiar faces weren't uncommon.

Since then Deputy Park had been reassigned to help Foster's search for Cole, and Millie had been given clearance by the sheriff to stick around Foster's office. There she'd decided to do what she'd become good at in the last six months.

She wrote down notes and created timelines, much like she'd done on the whiteboard in her kitchen at home.

If Foster's feeling was right—that it was the two of them who had stumbled onto another investigation entirely—then assuming everything so far had been connected was as bad as assuming everything wasn't.

Millie was now looking at Fallon's name,

which she'd put in the middle of the paper. Arrows branched off from his name in several directions.

If Millie and Foster really were putting a kink in someone else's investigation, then what did that mean for Fallon?

How was he involved?

If he was, why hadn't he reached out to her?

And where had he been?

The cold and creeping worry that Fallon had found something worse than trouble pulled Millie's heart down.

Just as quickly she shook her head to get rid of even the possibility that Fallon's truck was in play because he'd been a victim.

You haven't thought like that in the last six months. You can't start now, she mentally chided herself, eyes focusing on the paper between her hands. *There's got to be something you're missing.*

Missing.

Millie tilted her head. A new thought entering.

If Fallon was involved, who was he involved with?

Jason Talbot? Donni or Wyatt? William or Cole Reiner?

Millie grabbed her purse and slung it across her shoulder. She left Foster's office with purpose and didn't slow until she found him leaving the interrogation room.

Even without speaking, she could tell his frustration had been turned up to extra high.

Still, concern lit his features at the sight of her.

"What's wrong?" he asked without preamble. "Did you find something?"

Millie didn't waste time either.

"It might be nothing, but there was a screen missing off one of the Rosewater's back windows when we were looking there the other day. Maybe that wasn't just bad maintenance." She lowered her voice. "We know that Reiner wasn't the one who took us since he was spotted leaving the bar before us, so whoever drugged us and took us from the bar had to be close, right? Did anyone from the department search the midsection of rooms at the motel? If not, can we?"

Foster shook his head. That frustration stretched into something else.

"No, but, Millie, Wyatt Cline just woke up and he said he wants to talk."

Chapter Nineteen

The hospital was quiet.

Somehow, that made being there exponentially more unsettling.

At least that's what Millie told him, shoulder against his as they walked side by side down the hallway and toward the elevator. Since their unexpected time together, he'd realized their orbit had gotten smaller around one another.

Little moments.

Leaning in toward her, touching the small of her back or her elbow to lead her in the direction they needed to go, looking at her when she was doing something else.

It was an odd feeling.

It also wasn't a logical one.

Foster had known Millie for a little over a week. Within that week they had been put in high-pressure situations that weren't run-of-the-mill by any means. Danger, fear and violence had created a bond between them. An understanding and relatable thread.

But when they found Fallon?

When they figured out what happened with Cole and William Reiner?

Well, Foster imagined they'd have to talk about what he and Millie meant to each other then and if that thread between them had severed.

Foster wouldn't be mad about it.

He'd been with Regina for a decade and known her for a decade more. She'd been a great woman and they'd had all the tools to have a great life together.

But they hadn't.

Foster knew deep down that that wasn't all on him, that they'd been too young when they'd married and then kept on with their mistake just to prove everyone wrong. Yet there had been another factor that had put pressure on their marriage.

Foster loved his job and, when it came to solving a case, to getting justice, he kept going until it was done.

Right now, that worked for Millie and him. She wanted to know what had happened to her brother and wanted justice for their abduction. The truth was, though, that Fallon wouldn't be his next case, nor the one after.

Would Millie still be accepting of his job then? Of him? Of his inability to let go?

Maybe you're the one who's trouble, Love, he thought to himself as they moved into the elevator. *Here you are with a lead and you're wondering if Millie will still want to kiss you after it's been followed.*

Millie, unaware of yet another series of thoughts pertaining to her rattling around in his head, eyed the elevator around them with blatant hesitation.

"What I like less than a hospital that's eerily quiet is a metal box that has the ability to plummet back down to the ground with me in it."

There Foster went smiling again.

"Just think of it like a car going uphill." He pressed the button for the third floor. He didn't say it, but he suspected the quiet of the lobby would disappear once they made it to Wyatt's room.

At least he hoped.

Any information Wyatt might give was probably more than they had.

Millie lobbed a side-eye at him. Warm amber.

"Watch out there, Detective," she said with a smirk. "You might make me afraid of cars too."

Foster mirrored the smile but quieted. When the elevator stopped at the third floor, there was a lag in the doors opening. Like a switch had been flipped, the teasing stopped.

"What if Wyatt doesn't know anything?" Millie's voice wasn't just small. It was broken.

Foster knew that that wasn't the question she really wanted to ask.

What if Wyatt knows something and it's not good?

A lack of answers had so far hurt and saved Millie. She had no idea what had happened to Fallon, which meant she could blissfully stay away from the worst-case scenario. Wyatt could keep her in the dark or he could shine the light on an uglier truth.

And there wasn't anything Foster could do about it.

"You don't need to be in there, Millie," he reminded her. "I'll repeat every word he says to me."

Millie shook her head. "We're a team," she said with purpose. "I want to be there. I need to be there."

The elevator doors slid open and they walked out onto the floor. At the end of the hallway stood the sheriff. He had waited for them.

"I didn't think we were a team," Foster teased, trying to diffuse as much of the mounting tension as he could before they were at Wyatt's room.

Millie played ball.

"We won't be a team long if you keep telling me things like pretend elevators are cars. Next thing I know you're going to tell me to imagine a clown the next time I'm at the dentist."

"So you're afraid of clowns? Or you're afraid of the dentist?"

Millie laughed. "If you value this partnership, then you'll avoid both topics."

"Fair enough."

The walk to the sheriff was a short one. All jokes and teasing were left at Wyatt's door. Sheriff Chamblin tipped his cowboy hat to both of them before taking it off all together.

"The doc said he's stable and not resisting or anything," he told them. "He wouldn't let me handcuff him, but he's had hospital security on him the entire time one of us couldn't be here."

"Good," Foster said. "Has he talked to you or anyone about what's going on?"

The sheriff shook his head. "Since he's not going anywhere and you're lead on this, I wanted to wait." He looked to Millie, then back to Foster. If he was about to try to talk him out of letting Millie come in too, he was going to have a hard time of it.

Thankfully, he didn't.

"I'll let you keep the lead on this," he said instead. Then he held the door open for him and Millie. "Let's get us some answers."

The hospital security officer gave them a nod as Foster, Millie and the sheriff set up in the room. They each took up a spot around the hospital bed. Millie to the left, the sheriff to the right and Foster at the end. Despite their closer proximity, Wyatt's gaze went to and stuck to Foster.

"Wyatt Cline, I'm Detective Lovett with the sheriff's department and I have a few questions."

MILLIE HAD SEEN Foster naked, felt him against *her* naked, yet seeing him command the absolute attention of a man who had tried to shoot him days before brought out a different kind of attraction in her. It was like seeing someone in his element and being in awe of him.

Respect mixed with admiration and a big pinch of passion added in.

It was easy to stand there, quiet, and watch him do his job. Even the sheriff remained silent as Foster dove in without further preamble.

"Why were you out on that boat?"

Beneath the fluorescent lights of the hospital, Wyatt Cline appeared harmless enough. He was round and young and had dark rings beneath his eyes. A young man who looked like he was working himself to the bone for some corporate bigwig and a promotion he probably was never going to get. And now he was in the hospital for it, an older man of the law ready to give him a stern talking-to.

He didn't fit the image of intimidating. He definitely didn't fit the image of Donni Marsden's partner in crime.

Wyatt rolled his eyes, only adding to the impression of youth Millie got from the young man.

"I'd always wanted to go night fishing," he responded, voice a bit on the scratchy side. "Seemed like as good of a time as any to try it out."

Foster stopped the story by holding up his hand.

"We heard everything you said before Deputy Park showed up. You were looking for me and Miss Dean. Why and how did you know where to go?"

Wyatt didn't respond this time.

It only made Foster lean in more.

"Wyatt, you pulled a shotgun out and aimed at a member of law enforcement. That's attempted murder, bud. It was also caught on Deputy Park's body camera so it's not just hearsay. It's a provable fact." Foster took a beat, letting his words settle in a little. "This conversation right now doesn't keep you from going to prison. It only decides on how long you'll be there. So, if I were you, I'd start cooperating while my patience is still intact. And let me tell you, after the week I've had, that patience is paper thin and only getting thinner."

All of the defiance and snark seemed to deflate right on out of the younger man. He shared a look with Millie and the sheriff before going back to Foster.

He came to a decision quick. "I want immunity," he declared. "Immunity or I don't say anything."

The sheriff spoke up on that. "We can only start to talk about talking about a lesser sentence if you give us actionable information, just so you're clear."

Wyatt didn't like that. Foster was quick to slide back in.

"That's the only shot at a good deal you're going to get during all of this, Wyatt," he said. "If that works out then, add in good behavior, and it could mean the difference of years."

Millie didn't know if that was necessarily true—she'd seen on cop shows where they'd stretched the truth to *get* the truth—but she found she didn't care at the moment. Wyatt knew something.

They needed to know that something too.

Wyatt gave them all another passing glance.

Then defeat was all that showed on his freckled face.

"Fine. I'll tell you what I know."

The sheriff pulled out a notepad and pen. Millie didn't mean to, but she took a small step closer. Foster, ever the detective in charge, stayed as sturdy as a statue.

"Why did you go out to the boat?" he repeated.

Wyatt sighed and surprised her yet again. He lifted his arm slowly and pointed in her direction.

"Donni called and said he'd heard that her and some cop had been taken. He said we could use that to finally get what we wanted."

Foster didn't miss a beat. "What was it that you wanted? And how would Millie help you get it?"

Wyatt was a little more hesitant. "We thought that since he was finally making a move, we could use that to force him into a trade for her."

"Who's he?"

This time Wyatt was the one who looked surprised.

"William Reiner," he said matter-of-factly. "Y'all were taken to the boat to be delivered to him. You know, he's the bad guy, right?"

For the first time, Foster faltered.

Millie didn't know why yet—or maybe she did—but her blood started to turn to ice in her veins. A creeping cold that began to freeze her in place atop the tile floor.

"Do you know who drugged and kidnapped us to take us to the boat?" he asked, recovering.

Wyatt gave a half-shrug, then flinched. For a moment Millie had forgotten they were in a hospital, talking to a former gunshot and coma patient still attached to hospital equipment and an IV.

"Never seen him myself but I'm guessing Cole Reiner, you know, his brother."

"We would have noticed if Cole Reiner had been around to drug us." Foster's voice had gone even. No inflection, just powerful monotone.

Wyatt shrugged again. "I mean, that's probably where June comes in."

"Say again?" the sheriff spoke up. "You're talking about June Meeks?"

"Yeah."

"And why would June drug anyone?"

Wyatt snorted. "Well, she was pretty hot and heavy with Cole before he 'disappeared.'"

Sheriff Chamblin looked at Foster. His jaw set. Hard.

He was angry.

He'd been the one to vouch for June and, Millie was guessing, he'd had no idea about her former relationship with the younger Reiner.

Foster, however, stayed on point.

"So you're saying that June drugged us so Cole could take us out to an abandoned boat in the middle of the creek. Where we would then wait for his brother to come and collect Millie. Why would William Reiner go through all of that trouble and why would he go for Millie?"

A monitor beeped.

Someone made noise out in the hallway.

Air came out into the room from somewhere.

Millie could have sworn she heard her own heartbeat.

"Donni said he guessed it was because, after all of this time, she was still poking around to find out what happened to her brother. She even got a new guy, you, to help her. Some hotshot detective from the big city."

Millie took a small step again. This time backward.

Foster didn't volley back a question quick enough.

She knew it then, right then, that he'd already finished the conversation with Wyatt in his head.

That he'd already reached the end of the road.

That he already knew that her brother hadn't left Kelby Creek at all.

"William Reiner didn't want Millie looking for Fallon?" Foster had to ask.

Wyatt snorted.

Actually snorted.

He shook his head. "Considering he killed Fallon, no, I'm guessing he didn't want her, or anyone else, looking for him."

There it was.

The end of Millie's world, coming from the mouth of a man with shadows beneath his eyes.

This time Millie could have sworn that, instead of her heartbeat, she heard her heart break.

Chapter Twenty

Millie spent a good while tucked into Foster's chest.

She didn't know how long, and she didn't care who saw. For a while it was just the two of them. His heartbeat against her ear, his arms holding her together.

But, then, Foster had to go.

He had a bad guy to catch, he had a mystery to solve.

He had to get justice for someone who had been unfairly taken.

Fallon.

Every time his name echoed in Millie's head, she felt like she was falling deeper down into a hole. She saw the man he'd been, the child she'd loved, and the person she'd hoped to see him become.

Happy, healthy, and no longer struggling beneath the weight of his past.

Then came the awful sense of despair right after.

The churning and curdling heat of anger and hate came next.

Millie let herself attach to those ugly feelings to get her through everything that had to happen next. Then? Later on? She would go back to that deep, dark hole and cry into it until there was nothing left to give.

So, while her eyes might have been red and swollen already, when Foster pulled her into an empty hospital room half an hour later, Millie's words were running on default mode. She looked up at the man who had caught her the moment Wyatt Cline had destroyed her world.

Those green eyes—which now Millie was sure reminded her of tall grass on a cool day—searched her face with nothing but empathy. He stroked her cheek and then dropped his hand to her shoulder. The pressure felt nice, comforting. At least for a second.

Then it was gone and Foster was talking.

"There's a few things I need to do, so Amanda is going to take you home and keep you company until I'm done. Is that okay?"

"Did Wyatt tell you anything else?" Millie's voice was hoarse. Not too badly but enough to remind them both that she'd sobbed hard for a bit.

Foster looked like he'd rather not say, but he surprised her and said it anyway.

"He said he works for Donni, but Donni answers to someone else. Wyatt swears he's never known who that is, but that the Reiner brothers took something of theirs that they need to get back."

"Something? Like what?"

Foster rubbed his hand along his jaw. Millie hadn't noticed the stubble that sprouted along it until now.

"I don't know. The easy guess? Drugs or money. There's not much else usually good enough to entice the aggression of drugging and kidnapping a civilian and a member of law enforcement."

"Donni and Wyatt wanted to trade me to William Reiner to get back their boss's drugs and or money," Millie stated.

"That's what Wyatt's claiming."

Millie shook her head. It wasn't meant to be a disagreement. Instead, it was more disbelief than anything.

"That's a long, winding way to go to just kill me," she said. "I don't understand the trouble of it all."

Or the senselessness.

Killing Fallon for—what?—revenge? Then trying to get Millie to keep her from getting answers?

It was the last few dominoes of tragedy falling, the first one to be pushed over being her father's death.

Foster's hands were back to positions of comfort. They wrapped around her upper arms and steadied her.

"I will get every person involved and every answer we need. Okay?"

Millie nodded. She believed him.

Which was why she wanted him to leave.

"And you can't do any of that while worrying about me," she said. "I'll go home with Amanda."

Foster didn't look relieved but he nodded.

"Deputy Calloway is already outside your house, and his partner will come in and check on you two every half hour. There's also an updated all-points bulletin out on Cole. And June, who the sheriff is personally very invested in finding considering what Cline said about her involvement in our abduction." He used his finger to gently push her chin up so that her gaze was fully wrapped in his. "I'll be home as soon as I've ended this."

Foster's kiss was brief. The feeling it stirred within her wasn't. When he stepped back and helped her out into the hallway, Millie realized she'd have to unpack the complicated emotions tearing her up from the inside.

But now wasn't the time.

Amanda met her at the elevator, blue hair bright and frown severe. She didn't say anything. Just put her arm around Millie's shoulders on the way down.

She didn't need to pretend the elevator was a car anymore.

Not after her worst fear had come true.

DETECTIVE LEE GORDON lived in a part of Kelby Creek that Foster was unfamiliar with. A hard feat, given the size of town and the fact that he'd been adventurous growing up within its borders. Yet while driving up the long, twisted dirt road that led to a surprisingly large one-story house with a field behind it and woods on either side, Foster had to reorient himself a few times. He knew roughly where they were but, as he got out, it felt like he was on an island.

Total seclusion.

Foster just hoped that didn't translate to a man who was as helpful to him now as he had been to Millie when working Fallon's case.

Fallon.

Foster had known there was a good chance that the conversation with Wyatt wouldn't go the way they wanted. Still, hearing him say that Reiner had killed Fallon… That had hit hard.

Mostly because he could tell Millie knew it was coming.

The more Wyatt spoke, the more Millie seemed to build her defenses. Her body language kept changing from the first word until the last.

Yet all of those defenses—mental and otherwise—hadn't been enough.

And all Foster could do was catch her when they had come down.

When the tears came, they'd come from six months of worry. From years of love. From a life that should have been lived to one that didn't seem possible.

Foster had seen it before throughout his career. He'd seen hope and devastation all within one conversation. Yet Millie's body shaking against his, racked with sobs, felt different to him.

Rage and anguish and protectiveness had vied for top emotional position within him.

He didn't want to just console Millie, he wanted to change the world for her.

Something the sheriff seemed to pick up on.

"Remember what you told me about Regina and why your marriage didn't work out?" he'd asked after Millie had taken a seat in the hall so they could have a private moment. Foster had been more than surprised at that remark, but he'd nodded. "Tell me again," the sheriff added.

So Foster had.

"We were restless and young and got married to get away. Then we wanted to prove everyone who had told us it was a bad idea wrong so badly that we became people who liked each other but hated being married to each other." Foster had looked at Millie then. She was out of earshot but still he quieted. "Regina never understood why I loved my job and why I couldn't give it up."

"And why can't you give it up?"

"Because every case I work is about someone else's life," he'd answered. "And it's hard to give up on a life."

The sheriff had clapped him on the shoulder and smiled. It was a quick thing, but Foster couldn't help but be reminded of his father.

"*That* right there is the reason why you're one of the best people I know," he'd said. "And why we're going to help her life by giving her peace about Fallon Dean's death."

It was a pep talk, true as true could be, and it stuck its landing. Millie giving him the okay to keep going down the rabbit hole only strengthened Foster's feeling of purpose.

Of determination.

That focus was now drenched into his every movement. He took his badge and gun and hopped up the front porch stairs two at a time.

Detective Gordon had questioned the lead suspect when Fallon had disappeared. Gordon's statement on William Reiner had been short and had said in less than one paragraph that William hadn't done it and was a good man. There was no mention of an alibi or reason to drop suspicion in Gordon's file. Just like there had been no mention of Millie and Fallon's backstories and why Fallon's note should have been in cursive.

The retired detective had been incompetent.

Now he was going to have to answer for it,

as well as where his former colleague William Reiner might be.

Foster knocked against the door, already feeling his face harden in anticipation of an ornery man. According to Deputy Park, Gordon spent most of his retirement golfing, hunting and frequently bringing a new date to the country club in the city. Being questioned by the detective in between those activities probably wouldn't be something he'd appreciate.

Then again, maybe it was Foster's feelings for Millie that were coloring his opinion of the man he'd never met.

Either way, the longer Detective Gordon didn't answer the door, the more frustrated Foster became.

He walked around the porch and peered into the open garage. A small, sporty car in fire-engine red sat inside. Retirement sure was looking good for the man.

Foster backtracked to one of the front windows of the house and looked inside. A curtain obscured the view. He took a moment to listen. When nothing and no one made a noise, he decided to take a better look around.

He went back down the porch steps and walked around to the garage. Foster unbuttoned his holster and kept his hand hovering over his gun as he moved past the expensive ride and to the door that led inside the house.

This time he didn't knock.

The door was splintered at the lock.

It had been kicked in.

The gun came out of its holster in a flash.

He should have waited or called in backup, but all he could think about was Detective Gordon being in danger. No matter how incompetent he was, it didn't mean he deserved that.

Foster pushed the door open while doing his best to be quiet. It led into a galley-style kitchen, long and narrow. Sparse but high-end. Metal backsplash and granite countertops. A double oven and a beast of a refrigerator. Foster's gut started to wake up, but it wasn't the time to listen to it.

He moved through the room and turned into the living area. Foster's mind went through two different tasks.

Details.

Leather couches, large, flat-screen TV, a bricked fireplace with a mantel of law enforcement memorabilia, a high-end sound system and an honest to goodness self-portrait of Detective Gordon in uniform.

Defense.

There were three exits that led out of the room. The one he'd come through, one to the left that led into a hallway and one straight ahead that led to the front porch and outside. No one stood in the room or at any of the exits.

Foster continued on his tour.

The hallway had four doors that branched off to make up the right side of the house. The first door was open and showed a bathroom.

It looked like it came out of catalog, same as the next room. Foster opened its door and would have whistled had he not been trying to keep quiet. It was a home office but unlike any he'd seen in real life. Not even the *sheriff's* office at the department was as decadent.

One wall was nothing but a bookcase. Half of it was filled with books while trinkets and knick-knacks were interspersed between. The desk in front of it was slick metal and glass, the computer on its top slim and expensive. Two armchairs were set up much like the standard layout at the department but, unlike the department, there was a small table between them with an ashtray, a cigar cutter and the ends of two cigars.

Foster stopped a second and listened again. He heard no movement anywhere else, so he did what his gut was whispering to do and went to the desk. There, with gun in one hand, he used the other to open the top drawer.

Paper, pens, thumbtacks. Sticky notes.

Nothing out of the ordinary.

He opened the second drawer.

It was empty.

The third drawer wasn't.

There were more office supplies. But a bundle

of black zip ties was what caught and kept Foster's attention.

It wasn't unusual for those in law enforcement to have them, even retirees, but, still, Foster's gut wasn't buying it.

He was about to go to the fourth drawer when the sound of a door squeaking made him pause. Footfalls from, he guessed, the bedroom.

Foster took a few long, quick strides to the side of the door, just in time to get out of view from whoever was coming. His grip tightened on his gun.

It could have been Gordon.

If it was, Foster should have announced himself.

He *was* trespassing.

But his gut had gone from whispering to yelling so Foster didn't say a word.

A good choice, considering the man who walked into the office and right past Foster wasn't the man who owned the house.

Foster raised his gun and pointed it at the newcomer as he got behind the desk.

"Move and I'll shoot," Foster warned.

To his credit, William Reiner remained calm.

"I told him I heard someone," he said. "He said no one would come out here because no one had done it before, but I've seen your résumé, Lovett. And I know you're better than that."

The footsteps came out of nowhere. Foster barely had time to spin around.

For the first time in his career, he hesitated. *Truly* hesitated.

The young man's face was busted and bruised.

Foster lowered his aim, despite self-preservation and years of honing his instincts telling him to do otherwise.

Instead, he said the first thing that came to mind.

"What in the hell is going on?"

THE WHITEBOARD WOULD have undone her all over again had Millie not already felt numb. It was like gaining distance from the hospital had put space between the awful truth of her brother being gone and her current situation.

Denial.

That's what it was.

Deep and reaching denial.

Amanda walked the line between being supportive in silence and asking if she could get Millie anything. Past that she split her time between hovering and talking to Deputy Waller, one of the two deputies who had been assigned to Millie until the Reiner brothers and June were caught.

It was during one of those conversations where Amanda was on the front porch with the man that Millie ventured into the kitchen with the idea of finding something sweet to lessen the pain.

Instead, she looked at one of the only things in the house that could take her denial and break it down completely.

The whiteboard had seemed like such a good idea after Fallon had disappeared. Sure, it didn't match the decor of the kitchen—or the house for that matter—but it had helped Millie straighten her thoughts, all leads and the timeline of what had happened. The story of Fallon's life, written by the sister who was willing to do anything to fight for his future.

Now the marker was a violent contrast, but Millie couldn't look away. She wrapped her arms around herself and traced the date that Fallon had disappeared through Detective Gordon's barely there investigation to side points listing Fallon's friends, his job and then to the people who might want to do him harm.

Kelby Creek, written in all caps.

Beneath it was Deputy William Reiner.

Or it used to be.

Millie took an uncertain step forward.

The name hadn't only been erased, it had been replaced. "Dobb's stockroom. Come alone."

The words spilled over into notes about the Kintucket Woods and would have raised alarm in Millie, realizing that someone who wasn't her had written them.

But all Millie could do was cover her mouth with one hand and touch the marker with the other.

Every new word was written in cursive.

Fallon's cursive.

Something she knew by heart.

"Hey, Millie?"

Amanda's voice carried in from the living room.

All at once Millie made a decision. She didn't have time to wonder if it was a good one.

"In here."

She managed to get to the edge of the kitchen counter and lean against it before Amanda and her blue hair came into view. Instead of repeating the question asking if she was okay, she kept to a more neutral route.

"Deputy Waller just had some food dropped off, and I was wondering if you were hungry. He's out on the front porch with a smattering of choices."

Millie was touched, but she was also working on her maybe-not-the-best plan. Guilt spread across her conflicted heart as she feigned exhaustion.

"Honestly, I'd really just love to lay down," she lied. "I haven't been getting a lot of sleep lately and, well, today's been a lot."

Sympathy pure and true wrapped around every part of the coroner. She nodded, understanding.

"You do what you need to do," she said. "I'll get Waller to bring the food in and maybe we can eat later when you're feeling up to it?"

"That sounds good. Thank you." Millie paused as she walked by. "I mean it, Amanda. Thank you for being so kind."

Amanda shrugged. "I've found it's easy to be nice to good people."

Millie gave her a small smile, and they went in opposite directions. She wondered if Amanda would still think she was good people when she realized Millie had sneaked out.

Because that's exactly what Millie was about to do.

Chapter Twenty-One

Dobb's Grocer always smelled like cinnamon.

Millie had thought that the first time she'd walked through its front door past the Help Wanted sign and she thought it now as she used her keys to sneak in through the back.

The bike she'd "borrowed" from a neighbor down the block was resting against the brick wall that extended across the back alley. Main Street might have been out front, but the small alley that ran behind the buildings felt like a world away.

So did the back section of the grocery store.

For a small town, Dobb's was quite large. The main store spanned two buildings and always had two cashiers and one manager out front. The stockroom was the first door once inside and ran the same length of the two buildings but was narrow and filled to the brim with boxes, crates and product not yet shelved. Past that were the doors to the freezer where the meats were kept and the break room and employee bathrooms. If you kept straight on then you entered the shopping section of the store, right between the medicine aisle and the small toy aisle in the main room.

If Fallon wanted to meet her, there was only one room in the building that would give him the best chance of privacy.

Millie paused outside the stockroom door, hand hovering over the handle.

That morning Fallon had been dead; now he was waiting for her in the stockroom?

Was it naive of her to think that was true or was she back to being hopefully desperate and walking into a trap?

While she was sure the note on the whiteboard at her house was new within the last few days, that meant that Fallon would have meant her to find it after he'd written it. Was she too late now?

Standing here won't get you answers, her inner voice said. *The only way through it is through.*

Millie looked around the open area between the back half of the store. A part of her felt overwhelmingly glad that Larissa was off and that she hadn't told Foster where she was going. Also that the manager's office was at the front of the store so the chance of Robert walking back and finding her would be slim. Same for whoever the two cashiers on shift were.

Millie didn't rightly know who they were other than they weren't Larissa. She had, admittedly, not had her mind on work for the last week or so. Her thoughts had, instead, run between Fallon and Foster.

Two men she felt she needed but for much different reasons.

Millie flexed her fingers. The weight of her cell phone in her back pocket was like an alarm that never went off.

It was like when she'd gone out to the Kintucket Woods. There was nothing but hope on this side of the door, and the last time she followed hope into the woods, she'd been pulled into a series of threats, danger and the unknown.

Was it the totally wrong move to risk it all for even the chance of finding Fallon there? Fallon in perfect health and William Reiner nowhere near them?

It was.

Millie knew that.

She also knew that if there was any chance at all that Fallon was waiting for her, she'd always choose to go.

So Millie opened the door and went inside.

The fluorescents buzzed to life and illuminated the long room. No one and nothing jumped out at her as out of the ordinary. Shadows scattered across the floor-to-ceiling metal shelves and the various packages and goods on each. Toward the back half of the room sat a stack of four pallets with empty, open boxes. It was a recycling pile.

Employees took it out only when it nearly touched the ceiling.

Millie approached the cluster of boxes, heart hammering away.

She already knew what was supposed to be on the other side of them—two lawn chairs and a pillow where their youngest employee sometimes sat and played on his phone when he was supposed to be stocking—but she hoped there was something else.

Someone else.

She held her breath and made her way around the pallet.

Fallon wasn't there.

No one was.

Millie let out that breath in defeat.

Maybe she'd just missed him or maybe he hadn't come yet.

Or maybe you're reaching.

Millie shook the thought out of her head and started to search the area. The toolbox beneath one of the chairs that housed the store's box cutters, a hammer, and occasionally a candy bar, was partially opened.

Millie dragged it out and pushed the lid up. A folded piece of paper with her name written on the top was the first thing she saw.

It was written in cursive.

Foster's cursive, much like the note on the whiteboard.

The message inside was short. "I'm okay. I promise."

And there it was.

Millie might not have known all the answers to what was going on, but that was enough hope to lift the weight that had been crushing her since Wyatt had spoken to them. A glimmer of light in the dark.

She could work with that.

Millie slipped the note into her pocket and felt new resolve flood through her. Now it was time to rectify her mistake. Foster needed to know what she'd found, she decided, pulling out her cell phone.

They were partners, after all.

Better intentions or not, Millie didn't get far.

"Where is it?"

Millie spun around at the new, deep voice behind her, instantly terrified.

It wasn't Fallon.

It wasn't Foster.

It wasn't even Aaron, the teen who did their stocking.

Much like in the woods, all at once Millie realized just how badly she'd messed up. Her desperation had led her into danger.

No one knew where she was.

No one but the last man she'd expected to see.

FALLON DEAN STOOD in front of Foster like it was the most normal thing in the world for him to be there. Like him, William Reiner and Foster were just three men socializing in a home office on a nice, warm afternoon.

Not at all like a man who had been missing for six months. Definitely not like a man who had been supposedly killed by a Reiner.

A Reiner who spoke up quickly.

"We can explain," he said.

Foster, who hadn't even entertained the thought that Fallon would be who he found in Detective Gordon's house, rebutted with the first thing that came to his mind.

"You better have a good damn reason why this one here has made his sister worry for the last six months."

Fallon winced, but that might have had more to do with the bruises across his cheek or his busted lip. He gave the older Reiner a look caught somewhere between guilt and anger.

It heralded in a new tone for William. One that oddly sounded fond.

Two seconds into the conversation and Foster was already reevaluating everything they had thought they'd known.

"He does," William said. "But I can only tell you so much before we start having to make decisions."

Foster took a step back so he could look at both men. He didn't like that he was outnumbered. He also didn't like that he was the only one who didn't seem to know what was happening. Still, he kept his gun down and aim away from both men. A part of him knew that he wouldn't have been able to point his weapon anywhere near the grown man Millie had basically raised.

It didn't help that there was no denying the resemblance between the Dean siblings. Fallon's complexion was a match to Millie's, along with his dark hair with some curl. His eyes, the same shape but a different shade of brown, searched Foster's expression with a curiosity that Foster bet the man carried with him always. A trait that, no doubt, was thanks to his father's influence and belief in always learning.

Still, just because he wasn't going to aim his gun at Fallon didn't mean he wasn't going to lob some accusations at him.

"It was you," Foster said, sure of it in that moment. "You were the one I fought. You took us from Rosewater and put us on the boat."

"Yes, he is but there's a reason—" William started.

Foster wasn't having it. "We're about to get really acquainted in a second here, bud," he interrupted Reiner. "I want Fallon to answer me now."

"Fine," the older man replied. "But make it quick, Fallon. We're in a hurry."

Foster let that one go simply because he wanted to hear how Fallon could possibly make what he'd done okay.

Millie's brother or not, he'd made some bad choices. Ones that could only lead to being arrested.

Something Foster should have been doing now.

Fallon let out a breath that was long and tired. Then he was talking a mile a minute.

"William asked you to meet him in the kitchen a few minutes after he left through the front door so no one would suspect that he was involved. That timed everything right for Millie who passed out pretty quickly from the meds. You too, but when we were loading Millie in, it was like you came back awake and ready to fight. It didn't last long but, obviously, long enough." Fallon motioned to the bruising. "It might not have been the best or well-executed plan, but we didn't expect you two to team up to solve all the mysteries."

"So you sidelined us."

Fallon nodded. "We needed you and Millie out of the way just for a little while, especially after Jason had already tried to hurt her."

"Kill her," Foster corrected. "Jason Talbot tried to take her, and then when she ran he tried to kill her."

Fallon tensed all over.

"Which is why when you two kept at it we made a less than ideal decision," William interrupted.

"To drug an innocent woman and cop and

dump them on a boat to only then get attacked by two criminals? Less than ideal is a less than apt description of that plan."

"We didn't know who was watching," Fallon told him. "We—"

"We don't have time to tell you all the details." William cut him off. There was palpable tension in his shoulders. Time was running out.

Foster just didn't know what for.

"Why are you two here?" Foster pivoted to his most current question.

"Why are you?" William threw back. It, like his body language, was filled with mounting anxiety.

Foster didn't see the harm in telling the truth. Something he hoped the other two men would reciprocate with more clarity than the vague explanations they were giving him.

"I was hoping to ask Lee Gordon about the statement he took from *you*—" he pointed to William and then thumbed back to Fallon "—about *your* disappearance after Wyatt Cline said *you* were killed by *him* for revenge six months ago." He reversed his motions. Both men seemed surprised.

"He said I was dead?" Fallon's worry showed in his tone of voice. Foster knew where this was headed.

"Yep. He told me *and* your sister that a few hours ago."

Both men cussed.

William Reiner walked around the desk, closer to them. Not at all worried about the gun still in Foster's hand.

"If Wyatt Cline woke up and is talking, then there's a good chance Lee Gordon is about to pull a disappearing act," he stated. "Which means if he isn't already gone, he'll be coming back to pack to leave soon."

"You're going to have to give me a lot more than that." Foster turned his gaze to Fallon. "Start with what you've been doing for the last six months and how Reiner here is involved."

Again, Fallon didn't get a second to even open his mouth to respond. Instead, it was William who answered.

"He's been helping me look for my brother, the only place we knew to look. Which brought us a whole lot of nothing until we ran smack-dab into trouble last week." A look of disapproval moved across the older man's face. It was aimed at Fallon. "When both Fallon and his sister decided to do something impulsive."

"Give me more," Foster ordered.

Fallon sighed. "I took a chance and stole something from someone I shouldn't have. Then apparently Millie went to the woods to look for me and found Jason instead."

The pieces, as wild and unpredictable as they'd been since Foster had met Millie, started to vibrate in his gut. Like magnets sensing their partner, getting ready to connect.

"That's why Jason went after Millie," he said, realization dawning. "He was trying to get back what you took? Then Wyatt and Donni went after it after Jason was killed?" He looked to William, who didn't correct or argue the questions. "Wyatt said that you'd want Millie for revenge because of your accident and that you would trade her for whatever it was that was taken."

William nodded.

"But Wyatt was under the impression that Fallon was dead and that Cole and June Meeks were helping you," Foster added.

He didn't miss that at the mention of Cole's name, William's expression turned pained.

"June helped us because she loved my brother, but…but Cole… He's not a part of this."

That didn't sound good.

Not at all.

Foster thrummed his fingers along the butt of his gun.

If he had misread the intentions of the two men too close to him in a small room, he'd have to act fast.

"What happened to Cole?"

A look passed between William and Fallon. The former gave the other a small nod.

Fallon let out a breath of regret. "After The Flood happened, Cole suspected that there was someone still dirty in the department who didn't get caught. Someone who had taken a lot of money through the years to doctor files and cover up certain misdeeds. But Cole didn't know who exactly that was and decided to try to find out on his own just in case." He gave another look to William.

"And he didn't come to you?" Foster asked the older Reiner.

That pained look sunk in his frown.

"Not every sibling pair can be as close as the Dean children."

Foster wasn't about to argue that as Fallon continued.

"Cole disappeared completely soon after he quit, and that's when William started trying to figure out what was going on. We never found Cole but a few months back heard talk that a former young deputy from the department had been killed for trying to stop a massive drug deal out in Riker County."

"Cole," Foster surmised.

Fallon nodded.

"So, how does Cole go from quitting to being in the middle of a massive drug deal several counties over?"

William took this question. "When Cole was new to the force, a friend of his was killed in a drug bust that, according to the file, his friend facilitated. The case always bothered Cole because he didn't believe his friend could do that, but it wasn't until The Flood happened that he questioned what actually went down. Cole started looking into every member of law enforcement and official involved in the case, all the way down to the coroner. Then he quit and then he disappeared. My guess is he found his way from who he suspected to the drug supplier who had supposedly sold to his friend who was killed. Then he died trying to stop them."

"So you *have* been investigating Cole's investigation," Foster said. "And we've been investigating Fallon, which ran right into you."

William nodded. "I tried for months to figure out where Cole was and who he suspected. Then one day I was drinking myself dumb when this one here showed up at my door."

Foster had been waiting for this. The connection between the man who supposedly hated Fallon the most and Fallon himself.

"It was the anniversary of his retirement and the paper did a story on it. Like a recap," Fallon said, taking over. "I realized, after all of the years, that I never actually apologized for my part in the accident. Or explained why I was out there at all. But when I showed up he was clearly upset about something else. And, well, he told me everything he knew and I offered to help if I could."

"And he did." William smiled. It was brief but genuine. "He gave me the idea to go a different route than my brother did to try and find the dirty cop. Instead of looking into law enforcement and town officials before, during, and after The Flood—"

"—you looked into the drug supplier's side," Foster concluded.

William nodded. "Everyone knew me so I couldn't ask a lot of questions without raising suspicion, but Fallon had a history and a town whose law enforcement largely disliked him. It was easy for him to dig deep in that side of life."

Foster couldn't believe it. "You left town to go undercover into a drug operation to try and find a dirty cop," he said.

Fallon shrugged. "When you say it out loud it doesn't sound as great but, yeah."

Foster put his gun into his holster and ran a hand along his jaw.

"And I'm guessing you didn't tell your sister because she would have shut that down really quick." He looked at William, realizing one of the errors of their plan that had led Millie and Foster into it. "You wrote the note, didn't you? You did it before he told you that he always writes in cursive to Millie."

William sighed. "Yeah. If we went back and fixed it, it would have only added more questions. So we left it alone and hoped to figure out everything as quickly as possible."

"Okay," Foster said after a moment. "Okay.

So there are still some more detailed answers I want, but I have to ask again, why are you *here*?"

"Because, dumb or not, what I stole finally gave us a name," Fallon answered. "Lee Gordon."

Foster should have been surprised but ever since he'd seen the sports car, his thoughts on the former detective had started to change from a man who was possibly incompetent to a man who might not be as cut-and-dried as he'd once seemed.

William motioned around the room. "You tell me if you think this house should belong to a single, retired small-town detective with no family money or investments to be had."

Foster couldn't, but he was ready to ask more questions when his cell phone started to vibrate in his pocket. It was loud enough that it drew the attention of two set of eyes. He answered without hesitation when he saw the caller ID read Dr. Alvarez.

Foster didn't care about Fallon or William or even Lee Gordon anymore.

All he could think about was Millie.

"What's wrong?"

Amanda didn't hesitate either.

"Foster. She's gone. Millie's gone."

Chapter Twenty-Two

The gun bit into Millie's back, pushing her out of the stockroom like she hadn't already wanted to leave it and the man holding the gun behind.

"Why are you doing this?" she cried out.

Lee Gordon was dressed like he should have been out on the golf course. He had on a nice button-down and slacks and brown loafers. None of which went with the gun or the severe anger marring his expression.

Anger clearly aimed at her.

"If you would have let that no good brother of yours go, none of this would have happened. But *no*. You, like him, are more trouble than you're worth."

Millie let out a small noise as Gordon pushed her through the door. She spun around but not before taking a few steps away for distance. The back door to the grocery store was behind her, but the door to the main room was closer.

Gordon held the gun up and stepped between her and the closest escape.

"I don't understand," Millie said again. "What do you want?"

It had been almost four months since Millie had seen Lee Gordon. She'd imagined on occasion that he'd be lounging on the couch, beer in hand, and watching TV, living stress-free and not thinking about Fallon ever again. He'd barely showed interest when he had the case, after all.

But standing there now, Lee Gordon looked like he hadn't enjoyed an ounce of his retirement. There were bags beneath his eyes, stubble along his jaw and a frown that seemed to drag his entire face down. He didn't look like the man Millie had loathed after he'd officially closed the investigation into her brother's disappearance.

"You know, I worked my tail off for *years* for the chance to not have to work at all," he said. "I did what I was supposed to and then I did a bit more, just so I could leave it all and not worry about a thing until the day I died. But then you show up and get everyone in a tizzy over a boy who wasn't even worth the gum on the bottom of a shoe *before* he got William Reiner mangled." He shook his head. "I should have said no to it, retired early, but I figured what harm would it do to just tell everyone what they already knew? That Fallon Dean was a runaway."

He took a moment, but the aim of his gun stayed on her. Millie wasn't near anything she could use as weapon. Her best hope was to hear the man's rant and try to stretch it long enough to find a way to escape *without* being shot.

Gordon laughed.

There was no humor in it.

"That's where I messed up," he continued. "I went to talk to Reiner and saw Fallon's truck under a tarp. Knew it then that he had killed the boy. Justice, if you ask me."

Millie's heart squeezed.

She clung to the hope that the note in her pocket had been from Fallon and not an elaborate hoax by Reiner.

"I guess it didn't matter if I reported it or not. Just being there must have put me on the younger one's radar."

"Cole," Millie couldn't help but say.

Gordon snorted. "I'd heard he was sniffing around former law enforcement, especially those who hadn't been caught up in The Flood. But it wasn't until I had some former acquaintances of mine show up, asking me to fix everything or else, that I realized just how close he'd gotten. That's when I had to outsource."

Millie didn't know why he was giving her a rundown but had to admit she knew from experience how cathartic it felt to vent. She also wanted answers.

"You're who Donni and Wyatt were working for?"

Gordon made a face. Like his laughter, humor wasn't the cause of it.

"Working for me would suggest they listen to what I say," he answered. "All they were ever supposed to do was get back the damn ledger that Cole stole from Jason *The Idiot* Talbot. But, no, they thought it was a great idea to step in the middle of whichever Reiner-sibling plan involved you and that overblown detective and a boat."

He shook his head with more force than before. Then he shook the gun at her.

"But if William wants you so badly, then I'm going to cut through all of this madness and deliver you myself. If he won't give me the book for covering up the murder of your whiny little brother, then I'll sweeten the pot with the opportunity to finally destroy all of the family that destroyed William Reiner's." He motioned his head to the back door. "The only choice *you* get now is to come quietly or I'll make a pit stop to kill your Detective Lovett, since I've heard you two have become so close."

Millie went from standing still, wondering what the heck the ledger was all about, to making another not-so-great choice that day.

She ran.

Right at Gordon.

It caught the man so off guard that he didn't

pull the trigger until Millie's hands were already pushing his wrist and arm up.

The shot exploded overhead and made an awful noise. Glass shattered. Someone in the store screamed.

Millie didn't slow down.

Her momentum took them both backward, much like her fight with Jason. This time there was no wall right behind them. There was also a gun in play from the get-go. The ground caught Gordon just as he squeezed off another shot.

Millie recoiled on reflex as the sound pierced her ears.

It was all Gordon needed to throw her off him.

She tried to scramble back but it was too late.

Gordon turned the gun on her—

Then yelled as a man tagged in and threw a punch that redirected Gordon's aim. The gun dropped from his grip and skidded across the floor.

Millie had hoped her savior was one of two men. Yet, as the newcomer turned, it was neither Foster nor Fallon.

"Cole?"

Millie had never seen Cole Reiner in person, but she'd seen his picture. There was no doubt it was him, dressed down but fiercely focused, and ready to tussle with the former detective.

When he looked her way and yelled, "Run," Millie decided to let him have that tussle.

She scrambled to her feet and ran half-bent and stumbling to the double doors that led into the store. Once on the other side, she was met by nothing but the sound of '80s music that looped on the overhead speaker and a commotion from, she guessed, the street. Any employees or shoppers must have run at hearing the obvious shots.

Millie was about to follow.

She tore through the toy aisle as another shot went off behind her.

She didn't have time to wonder where it hit.

The sound of squeaking tennis shoes against the recently buffed floor shot another dose of adrenaline into her veins. Someone was coming toward her from the front of the store.

More than one someone.

Millie stopped and readied to pivot, going back a few feet to the midstore opening that cut across the middle of the space and aisles, but she ran out of time.

She watched, heart in her throat, as the two people she'd wanted to see most came into view.

Foster looked her up and down in an instant. He held his gun down at his side, and focus unlike any she'd seen yet was evident across his features. He ran toward her, saying something, but Millie didn't hear it.

Her own focus homed in on the man who she'd been told that morning was dead.

But he wasn't.

A look of relief and guilt washed over Fallon's face.

If Millie had the time, she would have cried right then and there.

Instead, the world turned to chaos.

Everything that had slowed when she saw her brother, alive and well, sped up in a whirlwind of violence and sound.

The three of them came together just as the doors to the back banged open.

Millie didn't look back but knew it wasn't good.

Another gunshot sounded.

Millie went from trying to run to being caught off guard as Fallon tucked himself around her. Both staggered as Foster yelled out.

One last gunshot went off, but Millie couldn't tell from where.

Instead, she fell to the ground beneath the weight of her brother.

The deadweight.

She held on to him as pain lit up her backside from hitting the floor.

Fallon wasn't moving but Foster was.

She watched in what felt like an out-of-body experience as the detective ran down the aisle and right up to Lee Gordon, his discarded gun and the blood around both.

Foster had shot him, just as he had Jason to protect her.

But this time, he hadn't been the one to take the bullet meant for her.

This time Millie did cry as her brother lay limp in her arms.

FOSTER SPENT A portion of his life not believing in good luck or bad luck, yet, three months later he was starting to decide it was okay to change his mind.

The bad luck had already happened, but no one realized how much until Foster had finally managed to get all parties together for a chronological and lengthy explanation of the last six to eight months.

And it had happened to the exact people who deserved it.

It was bad luck for Lee Gordon that, after years of helping a drug supplier in exchange for cuts of the money—which he had used to live an expensive lifestyle after retiring—that he'd covered up the death of none other than Cole Reiner's childhood friend. A man Cole had decided to avenge by getting justice, even when it included dropping off everyone's radar to find whoever was the dirty cop.

It was bad luck that William Reiner, who had realized the value of family in the last few years, had become so determined to find his little brother that he'd accepted the help of another little brother who had been looking for redemption.

It was bad luck again when both parties, looking for the same dirty cop, had gone about it by opposite routes. Cole had learned everything he could about those who had been a part of the corruption of The Flood and those who had managed to run from it while William and Fallon had infiltrated the drug scene that stretched across South Alabama to find the exact supplier who had worked with the same dirty cop.

It was bad luck that Millie Dean had refused to give up on her brother, no matter what anyone said, which led both to her and eventually Foster to confuse all sides involved.

And it was an extra dose of bad luck that Millie and Fallon had both missed each other so much near the six-month anniversary of him leaving that both had made impulsive choices.

Fallon had befriended and then stolen from Jason Talbot the one piece of evidence that eventually led to proof that Gordon had been involved in several transactions, deals and cover-ups, while Millie had gone to the woods, making Jason think she was working with her brother.

Everything else that had followed eventually turned into good luck for everyone who deserved it in the end.

William Reiner was reunited with his brother and Cole was able to provide leads to several cold and closed cases that had potentially been tampered with before The Flood happened. He also accepted a job back at the department with every intention of going for detective in the near future. June, his now fiancée, had been beside herself at his homecoming. So much so she'd announced she was ready to go to jail for drugging Millie and Foster.

It was an admission no one accepted and the only area of transparency everyone involved believed could stay a little opaque.

Then the focus turned to Fallon.

For all the trouble he'd put Millie through, Foster should have felt some anger at the young man. Yet the moment Fallon had shielded his sister from Gordon's last shot in the grocery store, Foster had decided he could never do wrong by him. He'd been as brave as his father had the day he'd shielded Fallon.

And it was only after Millie realized that Foster had given her brother the Just in Case bulletproof vest to wear before they'd gone into the store, that she pulled Foster down to their level with a strong embrace and a passionate kiss.

The good luck had continued from there on by way of the town, county and state covering the intricate story of two sets of siblings fighting for justice and each other with the help of the sheriff's department. It didn't make anyone forget about the town's past, but it was a step in the right direction.

"Keep it up and we might turn this place around yet," the sheriff had told Foster on the way out.

Foster aimed to do just that.

But not without doing a few things first.

Foster parked outside his house but walked up his neighbor's drive instead.

The front door opened before he could knock.

Fallon was grinning. "I'm not supposed to say anything yet," he confessed hurriedly in a whisper. "But Millie just got accepted. Full scholarship. She told me it wasn't a big deal but when she tells you, make sure to hype it up."

Foster did a little dance of excitement. Fallon joined in. After the world had settled around her, Millie had decided that she wanted to become a social worker and had applied for an online program that, according to her, was exactly what she hoped to get.

"I love where I am right now," she'd told him. "And I love the people I'm with. If I can do both, I'd like to try."

Now Foster didn't need to promise to be excited for her. He genuinely was.

Both men went quiet as Millie herself appeared in the doorway. She leaned in for a kiss that Foster turned into a dip.

"And that's my cue to go gag inside," Fallon said around a bite of laughter. He went inside and told Larissa and Amanda, loudly, that his sister was making out with her boyfriend on the front porch.

Millie shook her head, smiling when the kiss was done.

"Are you sure you want to switch houses with him?" she asked for the fifth time that week. "Living with me and having my brother as a next-door neighbor? That's almost a comically bad idea."

Foster grinned. "Don't you know? I eat bad ideas for breakfast."

Millie rolled her eyes. "The only thing you eat for breakfast is scrambled eggs with spoons because, for whatever reason, you keep throwing away your forks."

He let out a howl of laughter at that.

"You caught me doing it *one* time and now I'm marked for life!"

"All I'm saying is that when you officially get all moved in, I'm going to make sure my forks are already counted up," she said, hands going onto her hips. "I will not stand a fork thief!"

Foster got a squeal out of her as he pulled her in against him. The kiss they shared next quieted them both in the best way.

He wouldn't say it for three months—the night they'd get engaged—but in that moment Foster knew one thing with absolute certainty.

His luck had changed for good the moment he'd met Millie.

* * * * *

Look for the next book in Tyler Anne Snell's The Saving Kelby Creek Series when Searching for Evidence *goes on sale in August 2021. You'll find it wherever Harlequin Intrigue books are sold!*

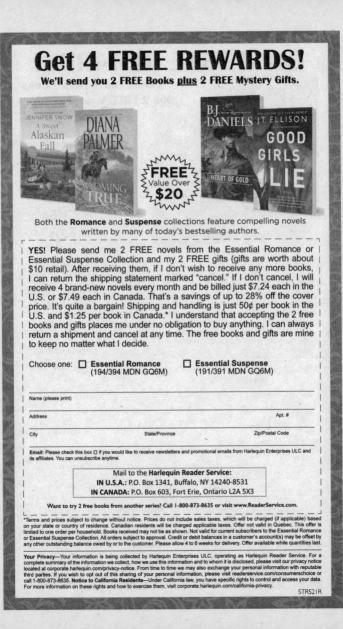